I0654586

THE LONER

Daughters of Destiny

K.R. GRACE

Liaison Publishing

COPYRIGHTS

The Loner: Daughters of Destiny, Book One

Written by K.R. Grace
    Edited by Grace McCammon

All Rights Reserved © Liaison Publishing 2014

This is a work of fiction. Any characters, names, places, or incidents are used solely in a fictitious nature based on the author's imagination. Any resemblance to or mention of persons, places, organizations, or other incidents are completely coincidental. No part of this book may be reproduced or transmitted in any form or by any other means without permission from the Publisher. Piracy is not a victimless crime. No individual/group has resale rights, sharing rights, or any other kind of rights to sell or give away this book unless expressly authorized by Liaison Publishing and the author.

TO MY BEAUTIFUL MOTHER

It is because of you that I am doing what
I love most: creating stories. Thank you for teaching me
that the only limits we have are those we place on ourselves.

PROLOGUE

৩⁂৩

Star

IN ORDER TO UNDERSTAND MY STORY, YOU NEED TO KNOW HOW it all began. So, sit down by the fire. Get comfortable, because this might take a while.

You see, there is this untold ancient Cherokee legend. They don't talk about it because it brings on a lot of shame and regret. Back when the Creator made the world, He sent a fleet of angels to protect the humans. This legion of angels was called *Guardians* and took on the form of animals so humans wouldn't be able to identify them. Something about people acting on their best behavior when authorities are around.

Anyway, the Guardians and the humans existed peacefully for a while and everything seemed to be great. The Creator gave twin sisters the respected task of leading the Guardians. They're names were Destiny and Fate. Destiny was awesome. Pure of heart and loved by all. Fate on the other hand was jealous and vindictive. Especially where Destiny was concerned.

After the great fall in Heaven, Fate saw it as her chance to become the sole leader of the shifters. Her goal was to destroy her sister once and for all. So, she created an army of fallen Guardians who'd followed the other fallen angels. They called themselves Shadowmen. Evil, vile creatures that preyed on innocent souls.

Fate sent the serpent shifter to trick the gullible humans into eating from the one tree the Creator forbade. However, she hadn't expected the Creator to react the way He had. All Guardians and Shadowmen were turned into humans who could take on animal forms.

Instead of being able to shift into any animal they wanted, each was assigned a spirit animal and given a specific task. Failure to perform the task or fulfill a purpose sentenced a shifter to an eternity on earth. Well, at least until the day of reckoning. A punishment worse than death because the human body is designed to pass on to the next life at some point.

To prevent another uprising, the Creator stripped away the shifters' ability to communicate with Destiny. Instead, only one shifter known as the Supreme Alpha could speak to her on the others' behalves. Originally, there were six Supremes, but one by one, Fate eliminated them, either by killing them or converting them over to her cause.

All except one who refused to bow to her and could not be killed.

A lone wolf.

He had an iron will and an unwavering loyalty to the Creator and Destiny.

Fate didn't consider it defeat, however. Instead, she got crafty. If the Supreme never passed on his title, then all communication between Destiny and the Guardians would end when he died. What was an army without its leader?

Fate devised a plan so evil, so horrible, all the lives involved were forever changed. Some for the better. Some for the worst. Three shifters' minds were altered so that they each were in love with the same girl. Only, this type goes beyond what you see in the movies or read in the books. It's a connection with another soul you are destined to love and when your mate dies, you die with them. Two hearts literally become one, and you are nothing without the other.

Three shifters, one girl. What could possibly go wrong?

Well, this is where I come in. Losing a loved one just sucks. Everything hurts. Nothing seems fair. And for a brief moment in time, death sounds like a good idea.

At least that's how it was for me.

Until a strange, wonderful guy came into my life and changed everything.

But even though I finally found my reason for living, for getting through the grief that weighed me down, I'll never forget the boy I lost. He was my first in every way except for the whole marriage and a baby carriage.

God, after all this time, just thinking about the night I got the news makes my heart hurt.

The rain was terrible. I mean it was like someone was trying to pressure wash the world clean of all that was dirty and evil. He and I were fighting, as usual. He was upset with me about something I'd done without consulting him.

He could be controlling like that, which was a sore spot for Mom.

I told him I never wanted to speak to him again, and I didn't want him to ever think of me as his girlfriend.

It was our routine fight that usually ended with us making up, professing our undying love for each other, and then doing it all over again. He stormed out like he always did, and I went into my room and cried into my pillow like I always did.

Three hours later, my phone rang.

I answered immediately thinking he was calling to make up, which he always did, but the female voice on the other end wasn't him. It would never be him on the other end again.

Clint was dead.

At first I didn't respond. I sat on the edge of my bed, my cell phone at my ear, listening to Clint's mother but not really hearing her. Words like "standing water," "hydroplaned," "telephone pole" and "died on impact" swam around in my head but weren't making any sense. I thought he was playing the joke of all jokes on me just to make me feel bad for what I'd said in the heat of our argument. Shock shifted to anger.

I said "goodbye" to his mother without asking any questions and called his phone to give him a piece of my mind.

But the call went straight to voicemail.

My parents tried to come into my room to check on me, but I wouldn't let anyone in. I didn't want to believe what they had to say. It was all a joke. Clint was going to call me and give up the charade. I kept dialing, listening to his automatic voice message, wishing he'd created a personal one like I always pestered him about doing, just so I could hear his voice and gain some false sense of reassurance that he wasn't dead.

He never called.

I was still in denial when my parents forced me to attend his funeral. The casket was open and he looked like he did when he would fall asleep on the couch while we were studying. I wanted to shake him, and wake him up so he'd stop the game and climb out of the coffin. When I walked up to him to say my last goodbye, I leaned over and pressed my lips to his cheek in hopes it would wake him up like in the movies.

I recoiled at the feel of his icy flesh.

Then the tears came. I was hysterical as I watched the pallbearers carry him out in his eternal cage and was inconsolable as they lowered his casket into the ground. I wanted to jump into the grave with him and have the undertakers bury me alive. I probably would've acted had it not been for my dad clutching me to his chest. I couldn't even make eye contact with Clint's mother. I was too afraid of what I might find there.

Anger. Disdain. Abhorrence because I was the reason her only son, her only child, was no longer alive.

My parents allowed me to miss a week of school in hopes I'd let out all my tears and start living my life again. A week passed and I still felt the gaping hole Clint left in my heart. We should've been soul mates, but he was dead.

I went back to school and was forced to endure the stares from other students. We'd been voted cutest couple in our grade. Everyone thought we were going to get married one day. I'd thought so, too. I guess I took love for granted.

I hated the whispers behind the hands, the sympathetic faces, and the ogling eyes. I just wanted everyone to leave me alone. My teachers were so understanding. Too understanding. My friends tried to be supportive, but none of them understood what I was going through. I felt cold, lifeless.

Months went by and my parents realized I wasn't getting better. They yanked me out of school and moved us out of our house in Atlanta to a small town I'd never heard of in Tennessee: Seymour.

My whole world changed in that tiny, godforsaken town. I met *him* there. How twisted is that? The greatest tragedy of my life led me to the best thing to ever happen to me.

So, how does this relate to the Supreme Alpha and the others? Well, here's how it happened.

❧ I ☙

❀

Star

SEYMOUR HAS THREE STOPLIGHTS, A POST OFFICE, A GROCERY store, a few debilitated restaurants, an industrial strip, one auto shop, a volunteer fire station, a small handful of fast food restaurants, and an even smaller number of gas stations.

That's it.

No movie theaters.

No malls.

Nothing.

I stared out the rain-speckled window as the tiny town flashed before my eyes, resigning myself to my prison sentence. What the heck did people do for fun around here? Go cow tipping and attend community dances?

Mom pulled into the parking lot of Seymour High School. She had a look of determination on her face that said I could protest all I wanted, but this was happening whether I liked it or not. God, I hated that face.

I begged her the night before to just let me be homeschooled. I mean, who transfers to a new school the last semester of their senior year? She didn't buy it.

"Why didn't you wear that pretty red shirt and blue jeans I set out?" Mom asked for the third time.

"Didn't feel like it," I mumbled.

"Honestly, Star. We understood when you decided to wear all black for a while but dying your beautiful auburn hair black just crosses the line. You look like one of those pot-head Goth kids."

I didn't call her out on her inaccurate stereotyping of all people who wore black. It wasn't worth the use of my vocal cords. She was always trying to get me to let go of my perpetual state of mourning. If no one else was going to grieve Clint's death, I would. I liked the pain, the void, the emptiness that could never be filled. It was my reminder and my punishment.

As we walked into the front entrance, I was greeted by a large yellow banner advertising cheerleading tryouts for the upcoming year.

"You should consider trying out. You know you were always good with gymnastics," Mom said as we passed it. Obviously she'd forgotten about my one and only competition. I took out the judges' table in my attempt to do a simple tumble. The incident landed me the nickname "Wrecking Ball."

I scoffed: my only source communication since...you know when. Even if I had the gracefulness of a gazelle and the flexibility of Gumpy, there was no way I was going to be the queen of pep. I just wanted to blend in so no one would notice me. It was the only way I was going to survive the last semester of high school without Clint.

We walked into the main office. A short lady with layered brown hair stood up and gave me the biggest smile I'd ever seen. It could've probably given Miss America a run for her money. It was overpowering and unnerving. I resorted to staring down at my black converse shoes to avoid her unending sunshine.

"Well, who do we have here?" the woman asked with a sugary

East Tennessee accent.

"I am Victoria Allistar and this is my daughter Elizabeth Allistar." Mom made the introductions.

"Do you go by Liz or Elizabeth?" the lady asked.

"I prefer Star," I muttered, not making eye contact.

"Star? Well, what an interesting name. I'm Mrs. Porter. Do you have your school records or did you have them sent from your previous school?" She was too bubbly for me. I mean, just looking at her was giving me a toothache.

"We had them transferred. My husband Tom got a new job in Knoxville, and we uprooted the family from Atlanta." Mom giggled nervously. She was a terrible liar. Dad didn't have a job yet. The move was because of me. Why they chose Seymour of all places was beyond me. It wasn't like we had friends or family in the area.

"Well, let me give you some papers to fill out, Mrs. Allistar. While you're doing that, I'll just take our Star here to the guidance counselor so she can draw up a schedule." Apparently Mrs. Porter found that funny because she giggled while she escorted me out. Seriously? Where did this woman come from? She was like a side character out of a Disney film.

I followed her endowed backside through a workroom and into a small room that had pamphlets in little holders mounted on the wall for how to overcome eating disorders and deal with teen pregnancy. It was odd; no one cared about how to get over losing someone.

The guidance counselor was okay. Not really the type of person I cared about being interested in on any level. Judging by all the trophies on the shelves lining the walls of his tiny office, he had to be the football coach. He definitely resembled a football coach: short and squatty with vague traces of his muscular-glory days in his otherwise flabby arms and fluffy chest.

"This is Star. She's moved here all the way from Atlanta." Mrs. Porter acted like we'd made the trek across America in beach chairs with helium balloons strapped to them.

He opened his mouth and said something, but all his worlds mumbled together, reminding of the teacher from *Peanuts*. I sat down in the chair he pointed to while he ran his beefy fingers over his keyboard.

If I squinted and turned my head slightly to the left, he sort of looked like Jigs, Clint's English bulldog.

Mr. Jigs-look-alike said a bunch of words I didn't understand, but judging by the paper he thrust in my hand, he'd decided I needed to challenge myself and placed me in chemistry II, calculus, Spanish II, and band.

"Sir, I can't play any kind of instrument. You can't put me in band."

"Grumble, mumble, wah, wah, grumble," was all that registered in my brain. If his lack of movement was any indicator, he wasn't going to change my schedule.

Just great.

I was staring at my schedule when he mumbled a few more words. Jerking my head up, I saw him pointing at the door.

Either he was releasing me or motioning for someone else to come in. A quick glance over my shoulder at the empty doorway told me it was time to go. So, without saying anything, I stood with my schedule in hand and let myself out.

God, these people are weird.

"Classes are already out for the day. Why don't y'all walk around, take a tour, find Star's classes, check out her locker." Mrs. Porter suggested as I joined her and Mom in the office.

I could care less about taking a tour of the school, but Mom tugged on my arm with a subtle pinch like she did when I was a kid, and we went in search of each class. The school was sort of shaped like an E with a tumor jutting out that was the gym and agriculture department. It was easy to find all my classes.

"We should go to the band room and see if the director's there. Surely there's an instrument you can play," Mom muttered as we headed down the hall. Unless using my recorder as a spitball launcher in my third grade music class counted as playing an instrument, I was musically disabled. So, this should be interesting.

Unfortunately, he was there, bent over a filing cabinet. He was a short man, leading me to the conclusion that people were just made shorter in Tennessee. His salt-and-pepper hair was cropped short and his cinnamon brown eyes were hidden behind wire-framed glasses.

"Hello, sir," Mom called to him.

He straightened with a lopsided smile on his face.

"Hi. What can I do for you?" He closed the drawer he'd been digging through before moving to join us.

"I'm Victoria. This is my daughter Eliz-uh, Star. We just moved here from Atlanta."

His eyes brightened and his smile kicked up a notch as he directed his gaze at me. "Is that right? What instrument do you play?"

"Um, I don't play," I muttered, not liking his enthusiasm.

"Oh, well, then what can I do for you?"

"The guidance counselor signed her up for the class."

"Of course he did," the director muttered. "Well," he said as he pasted a fake smile on his face, "I guess that means you're in band. I'm Mr. Thomas."

"Star McCallistar," I garbled as I shook his extended hand.

"Why don't we just put you in the percussion section for now? You can start with the triangle and work your way up from there."

"Whatever." Did I really have an option?

God, I was so miserable. Mom and Mr. Thomas chatted like old friends for thirty minutes about who knows what before she finally made her excuses to leave.

Once we were back in the car, I slouched down in the passenger seat, prepared to sulk the entire way home. To say I was unhappy would be an understatement. This whole move was supposedly for my benefit, and yet I felt worse than when we were in Atlanta. Mom was oblivious to my emotions. This was all about her and Dad.

Case in point, she blathered on and on about how wonderful the school looked and how nice the band director seemed as she drove us home. I pulled out the headphones to my iPod and put them in to listen to the next song on my playlist. It was a sad song. They were all sad. I'd intentionally removed anything joyful from my life.

When we pulled up to our new home five minutes away from the school, Dad was waiting for us in the driveway with a smug look on his face.

"Great news! I got hired as a crew manager at Dollywood!" he exclaimed as soon as we climbed out of the car.

"Oh Tom, that's wonderful!" Mom sighed and hugged him.

I didn't see what there was to be excited about. Who wanted to work in some lame theme park centered on the "country" way of living? I shrugged and walked passed him, never making eye contact. I didn't ask him to give up his VP position to move to this hick town.

I dodged the still-packed boxes in my room and sat down on the mattress in the middle of the floor. Nothing was normal. Nothing was okay. I just wanted everyone to leave me alone.

I pulled the hood of my hoodie over my head and plopped back onto the naked bed. Two hours later Mom knocked on the door.

"What?" I muttered.

"Dinner's ready."

"I'm not hungry."

"Please, you have to eat," she pleaded.

I almost felt bad but I didn't move, didn't respond.

I waited until the sun set and my parents were asleep before I went into the kitchen and dieted on canned cheese and chocolate chips. I no longer cared how I ate. I just consumed whatever sounded good at the moment.

I used to be a trained cross-country runner, well sort of trained. I was on the team but never won anything. My family had PTB syndrome (potential to bloat), so I'd avoided anything that might cause me to expand like one of those sponge pills that start out looking like medicine capsules and puff out into dinosaurs and bears when inserted in water.

Thinking about cross-country and dieting reminded me of my cross-country tryout.

As I leaned on the granite counter top, memories assailed me that I didn't want but was unable to hold back. Clint noticed me for the first time that day.

He had been my world. How does a girl live after her very existence is ripped from her so unexpectedly?

I remembered being nervous. Clint was a year ahead of me and already on the track for practice. It was a big deal to tryout. Only the best of the best made the team. It'd taken me forever to change because I checked and rechecked everything to make sure nothing was out of place. When I finally joined the other cross-country hopefuls, I heard deep male laughter and turned to where the men's team was doing warm-ups. The owner of the laugh was this cute guy with short blonde hair, bright sea green eyes, and the sexiest grin on the planet who just so happened to be in my geometry class.

Clint Blackstone.

Instead of using the low chained-link fence as a stationary hurdle like the other girls were doing, I decided to take the safer route and walk around to the gate entrance. No point in hurting myself on my first day.

Seeing Clint on the ground doing cross-legged pushups distracted me just a little bit. Okay, so maybe my brain was trained on him like a dog staring down a big, juicy steak. A big, muscle-bulging, sweat-glistening, mouth-watering piece of grade A beef.

The sun reflected off the golden hair on his arms and legs with every rep he did, mesmerizing me as he dropped down to the ground and pushed back up. Where it would've taken every ounce of concentration I had to do a one-legged pushup, he made it look effortless as he joked around with the guy next to him.

One second I was straining to hear what they were talking

about, and in the next my legs slammed into the fence and I went airborne. I flipped over the chain-link and landed hard on my back. All air fled from my body, and for a second I thought I'd died and gone to heaven when the sea green eyes I'd been obsessing over just a few moments ago came into my view. Suddenly, my lungs began working again as my heart kicked into overdrive, and I drank in my first painful breath.

"I'm going to take a wild guess and say you're not trying out for the hurdles," he joked as he extended a firm hand toward me. The way his muscles corded down his arms was a sight to behold. He wasn't Mr. Bodybuilder, but he definitely was toned...all over.

I smiled sheepishly and took his offered hand. The moment our fingers met I knew I was supposed to love him. I wasn't sure if we would ever get married, but I knew he was supposed to be my first love. My heart skipped a beat as he tugged me up into his arms and flashed me one of his heart-melting smiles.

"Don't worry, Legs. I've got you."

⊙⁊⊙

"You're still up?" Dad broke into my thoughts.

"Yeah, getting something to eat," I shrugged and pushed off the counter. I shuffled back into my room without giving him a second glance.

I sank down onto the mattress and curled up into a fetal position. I didn't sleep. I was too afraid of what the dreams would bring. Clint was always in them asking me to help him, but I couldn't. I lost him over and over again until I woke up shaking with torturing sobs that wracked my body.

⊙⁊⊙

I used to be the straight "A" student who obsessed over every grade and more often than not was the one who ruined the curve for everyone else. Now I just wanted it to all be over, to get my dumb diploma and be finished. What was the point in trying so hard when in the end, a diploma was a diploma no matter which way one looked at it. Unless one planned on going to college, which I didn't.

I sat down in the first available desk in my chemistry II class and tried to disappear into my surroundings. Unfortunately, I was a victim of the "new kid phenomenon." All the girls assessed me to determine if I posed a threat to their current social status while the guys decided if my fresh meat was worth pursuing. If I was lucky, the answer would be "no" on both accounts and everyone would leave me alone. Unfortunately, Lady Luck was never on my side.

"Elizabeth, would you like to introduce yourself?" Ms. Rickles the science teacher asked.

"It's Star, and no I don't," I said and slouched lower in my seat.

"Well, Star, it's nice to have you."

"She tends to be a little nosey. Don't mind her," a girl to my right leaned over and whispered.

Maybe if I gave her the look that said I thought she was an enigma rather than a human, she'd leave me alone. It didn't even faze her. She just smiled brightly and sat back in her seat. She was the peppy type with big blue eyes and shiny blonde hair pulled back in a ponytail. The bright Pepto-Bismol pink peasant shirt she was wearing was blinding my eyes.

Ms. Rickles spent the entire class period going over chemical compounds, something I learned in chemistry I, so I spent most of the time staring out the window overlooking the back parking lot.

My eyes immediately gravitated towards a guy wearing all black strutting across the lot as if he didn't care he was already an hour late. I leaned forward in my desk to try to get a better look at his features. There was something different about him. His muscles were larger than the average guy and he seemed taller too. His black hair was thick and hung just above his strong shoulders, giving him a rough-around-the-edges look.

As if he knew I was staring, he cocked his head in my direction and our eyes met.

Damn, I wished I was closer so I could see what color his eyes were.

Was he really looking at me? Or at the window? Or something else?

I got the instant vibe that he didn't allow people to get close. Of course, it only made me want to get a closer look at him. I wasn't sure why I even cared. It wasn't like I'd allow myself to be interested in anyone anyway. I was only allowed to have one real love in my lifetime.

The guy finally disappeared beyond my line of vision, and I slumped back into my chair. I spent the remainder of the class coloring in the lines of my notebook paper with my black pen.

I was relieved when the bell rang. Rather than shaking the annoying girl off, however, she followed me down the hall. I seriously did nothing to encourage her yet she acted like we'd exchanged phone numbers and swore to be each other's best friends forever.

"What kind of name is Star? I mean, did your parents give it to you or what?"

Maybe if I didn't respond to her, she'd go away.

"I'm Wayley, by the way. My parents say they just made it up. I think it makes me unique. Have you been here long? There isn't much to do. We usually have to drive to Knoxville, Pigeon Forge, or Gatlinburg to have some decent fun. I like your outfit. You must be from the city. What's it like living in a big city? I've always wanted to live in a big city. You have shiny hair. I wish mine looked like that. You wouldn't believe how much hair product I have to use each morning just to get mine to look like it does right now."

I wanted to tell her she was acting like Miss Bates from Jane Austen's novel *Emma*, but I wasn't sure she'd get the reference, or that it wasn't meant as a compliment. Instead, I made a sharp turn into my Spanish II classroom.

"Oh, I'm taking French. I'll save you a seat at lunch, though."

I'd never been happier to suffer through past predicates in my entire life. When the bell rang all too soon, I grabbed my things and regretfully left the classroom. She was somewhere in these halls. I could feel her. It was quite possible she somehow put a tracking device on me.

When the cafeteria came into view, I dodged behind a big dude with dreadlocks in hopes of going unnoticed. I didn't know how much I could take listening to Wayley. I mean, seriously, people like her ought to come with a mute button on them. I was so close to sweet freedom when I heard that unmistakable voice.

"Star! Over here!" She waved at me and the cafeteria went quiet.

Once again, I found myself under the microscope. Everyone was trying to decide what category I belonged to and whether I was an endangerment to their current social ranking. Newsflash to all of them, I didn't want to have any rank. I just wanted to be one of the loners nobody remembered. Unless they were afraid my dark cloud of doom would destroy the school's peppy vibe, I wasn't going to be a threat to anyone. I definitely didn't want to tip off the queen bees and kings of campus. The school would remain theirs as far as I was concerned.

Maybe I should've said that in chemistry so word would've spread by now. I sat down next to Wayley just to get away from the spotlight.

"Who do we have here?" a slender guy with a thick head of ash blonde hair asked from across the table.

"Guys, this is Star. Star, the guys," Wayley made the general introduction.

"I'm Chris," the blonde introduced himself.

"I'm Giles," a guy with ebony skin and a shaved head smiled.

"I'm Onyx. My parents are scientists," a girl with dark brown eyes and black hair smiled with a shrug. She reminded me of my friend India back in Atlanta. Her parents were doctors from Israel and had a wry sense of humor in naming their kids after other mid-eastern countries. Her brothers' names were Iran, Turk, and Sri (for Sri Lanka). I hadn't felt anything for the friends I'd left until I looked at Onyx.

"So, Star, where're you from?" Chris asked.

"Atlanta." I avoided making eye contact. He had the aura of a guy who was interested, and I wasn't interested.

"Oh, no wonder you dress so cute. It's very New York," Wayley began to babble.

Did she realize New York and Atlanta were as similar as apples and eggs?

"Yeah, we should so go shopping together. We can go to the outlet mall in Sevierville. It'll be fun," Onyx smiled.

I wanted to tell her the day I went shopping with them was the day the earth stopped revolving around the sun. Instead, I kept my mouth shut. Well, metaphorically at least. I merely chomped into my peanut butter sandwich.

"Oh, that sounds like fun," Wayley nodded.

"So, are you single?" Giles asked.

I didn't look at him, didn't even move. What made him think he could ask me that after only knowing me all of five minutes? Did I look like I'd welcome that kind of question?

"Giles, leave her alone," Onyx slugged him.

"What? I was only asking because I want to make sure no big dude is going to come and pound my face into the ground for looking at his girl the wrong way."

"Oh, shut up. You're such a dork." I heard Onyx snort.

I just sat there, staring at my hands. The panic was starting to creep in. All I could see was Clint's smiling face and hear his deep booming laugh. God, I needed to be wrapped in his arms so badly my body ached all over.

"Aren't you going to eat anything?" Wayley put her nose into my business again. Did she miss the lone bite of my sandwich I'd just taken before Giles sucker-punched me with his question?

"I'm not hungry," I shrugged, shoving my sandwich back into my bag. If the bell didn't ring soon, I was going to hide in the bathroom until it did. There was only so much I could take before I exploded on these people.

"First day jitters? I understand that one. I was new here three years ago," Chris said.

"Do you remember when Valeria Lewis moved here from Canada? Everyone flocked around her like she was some kind of rare diamond. Within a week she was dating Tyler Mitchum, the all-state quarterback," Wayley giggled.

Where was that blasted bell?

Finally, the bell rang, and I was released from my perky purgatory. I dodged the massive crowd in the main hallway and found my calculus class without a problem. I thought I was safe, until I heard the voice behind me.

"Imagine that, we all have calculus together."

God, the secret service could use the girl's voice as an interrogation tactic. They'd have terrorists spilling their guts within seconds.

I turned around to see Wayley, Onyx, Chris, and Giles. The only reason I didn't groan was because I was afraid someone would ask me to explain myself, or consider it an invitation to strike up more conversation. I must've done something horrible to deserve this kind of punishment. Maybe if I flipped them off they would get the hint. But, Wayley would probably think it was what all the cool kids in Atlanta did and the message would be lost on them. If I survived this, I was going to kill my mother for making me move here. At least back home people left me alone because they already knew the story.

The teacher came in and they were prevented from talking for the next ninety minutes. There was a God!

Mr. Nickelson might as well have been speaking French for all I was paying attention, but by the end of the class, I'd come up with a million ways to axe these people off and get away with it. Hypothetically speaking of course. Orange definitely wasn't my color.

When the bell rang again, I tried to shake them off by

scooping up my books and darting out the classroom like I was about to wet myself if I didn't get to a bathroom soon, but Onyx stuck with me like Velcro.

"I didn't know you were in band. What instrument do you play?" she asked as we walked toward the band room.

"The triangle."

"Oh, well, that's nice." She gave me a look as if to say, "Who specifically plays the triangle?" Thankfully, she kept her comments to herself. A first for her and her friends.

The sound of random instruments playing violated my poor eardrums as soon as the door opened and we walked into the band room. God, the place smelled like moldy feet and peanuts. There were two guys using purple color guard flags as light sabers. Another dude was doing some sort of jig while playing his trombone. I spotted the percussion section and everything in me screeched to a halt.

Sitting at the piano was the guy from the parking lot. He was playing as if he didn't hear the animalistic chaos going on around him. He'd pulled his jet black hair back into a short ponytail just off the nape of his neck, but one errant strand hung over his right eye. I stared at the muscles in his arms, watching them flex as his fingers effortlessly danced over the keys. Oh, but he was so mesmerizing. How he could be so large and yet move so gracefully was beyond me.

"That's Drake Knight. He's nice enough once you get him to talk to you, but he has a reputation for being...tough, if you know what I mean. They say he was part of this bad motorcycle gang. That's how he got hurt. The rumor is he was racing someone drunk in the mountains and went off the side into the water," Onyx answered my unspoken question.

He stopped playing and turned to pull himself up with metal crutches I hadn't noticed before. But, hadn't he been walking into the school just fine earlier?

The padded clamps slid over his forearms and he moved with awkward grace (if that's even possible) to a large table with wooden teeth. He sat down on a stool and leaned his crutches against the wall. I knew I was staring like an oaf, but I was helpless to do anything else. Did his problem only come around at a certain time of day?

I shook my head to get my brain working again before I moved toward the general vicinity of the percussion instruments.

"Hey there, did it hurt?" A tall, skinny guy with blue hair asked as he walked up to me.

"Huh?" I frowned. Had I missed something?

"When you fell from heaven. Because you're the prettiest angel I've ever seen."

"Don't quit your day job, kid." I brushed passed him to get to the table that held an assortment of noise-making instruments.

I could hear guys laughing and ribbing the smurf for being shot down but didn't bother looking at them. Instead, I scanned the contents on the table until my eyes finally landed on the triangle-shaped piece of metal on a string and the little metal stick next to it.

I turned and tried not to stare at Drake again, but his arms moving as he beat sticks on the wooden teeth drew my attention to him. Arms like his had to give really good hugs. Just the sight of them made me feel safe. That is, until I realized he was staring openly at me, his calculating yet warm blue eyes following me like a wolf stalks his prey. I quickly averted my gaze and acted like I didn't notice but I did. How could I not?

He made me feel like the frog Clint and I dissected in biology. We'd cut it open to find it overflowing with eggs. The teacher got so excited she had everyone stand around us and watch as we struggled to clear away the black goop to get to the organs. Said goop that, had the mother not been killed for the purpose of science, would've one day turned into bug-eating frogs.

That's how I felt. Like Drake was staring at my insides, taking away something vital in me that I wouldn't ever get back.

Weird.

Mr. Thomas started the band in what sounded like a stair of

notes. I didn't learn until the end of the year that it was called a "scale" and there were twelve major scales plus a whole bunch of other special ones. Thank goodness I only had to worry about one note.

Drake never took his eyes off me, even when we worked on the music...well, when *the band* worked on the music. I sat on my stool hopelessly lost. When the bell finally signaled the end of the day, I'm pretty sure I almost wept for joy.

Mom was waving me down in the parking lot. As if it was even possible to miss her bright red cat sweater. I honestly didn't care about what others thought of me, but I really didn't want the label given to seniors who still got rides from their mothers. The driving code in high school was simple. As soon as you were of age, you either: (a) drove yourself to school, (b) walked to school, or (c) got a ride from another student who could drive to school. There was no (d) none of the above.

I dashed into the car as quickly as possible. God, if kids got wind of Mom and her animal sweaters, it would totally kill my dark vibe.

As Mom drove off the parking lot, I spotted Drake leaning against a silver Jeep with its cover off. He looked so casual: legs crossed at his ankles, arms locked in front of his chest, and his blue eyes hidden behind aviator sunglasses. How could he stand so relaxed like that if he really needed crutches? Even though I couldn't see his eyes, I knew he was staring at me. I felt powerless and it scared me more than I liked to admit. I wasn't supposed to feel anything anymore, but around him it was like all my emotions were starting to come back to life.

The second we left the school property, all the heartache came back tenfold. My chest constricted violently as I drew my knees up to my chest, staring blankly out the window as tears fell down my face. Unwanted memories wrapped around me, pulling me back into the darkness.

2

Drake

I SHOULD'VE KNOWN SOMETHING WAS UP WHEN I CLIMBED OUT of bed without the aid of my crutches. It'd been a close call when a kid from my anatomy class caught me waltzing into school sans the sticks. One weird look from him reminded me I needed to be careful with how I transitioned back to "normal." It'd been a while. Almost forgot how good it felt.

What the hell was she doing here?

Damn, but she was beautiful. Her black hair hung around her pale face and her large, haunted green eyes stared at me like I was the only person in the room. It wasn't until she realized I was returning the favor that she suddenly got shy and avoided all eye contact with me. A very strong part of me wanted to grab her and take her as far away from here as possible.

She'd seen me walk into school without my crutches. Her thoughts screamed her confusion so loud it was hard to focus on anything else. I couldn't fix things now. I just prayed like hell I hadn't completely turned her off. If she thought I was pulling one over on everyone pretending to be crippled, she'd hate me. I didn't have to know her to know she was one of those rare people in this world who demanded truth and honesty from every person she came in contact with.

There had been talk in the pack that Helena's descendants were back. I hadn't given it much thought since the last time I saw her she was dead in a ravine. The legend died with her. Descendants were impossible. Right?

It didn't matter who she was. I needed to distance myself from her. I didn't do the right thing last time. Now that Star was here, I had a chance to fix things.

When Star and her mom drove past my Jeep in the parking lot, I specifically made sure I was in her line of vision. There was something different about her. I saw the resemblance to Helena instantly in those green eyes, but Star had a restrained strength Helena hadn't possessed.

I pulled out my cell phone and dialed Meliena as I drove off the lot.

"I told you she was coming," Meliena answered immediately.

I sighed as I struggled to hold back my sharp retort. Meliena was a great friend, but she had a tendency to throw salt in gaping wounds. "I don't need the 'I told you so' crap, Liena. I need to know what I'm supposed to do now that she's here and I've seen her."

"Did you feel the pull with her like you did Helena?"

"More than before."

"Okay. I think we need to have a meeting and decide where to go from here. If she's anything like Helena, she'll drag this out until it's too late."

"I agree about the meeting. Call everyone down to the cave. I need to stop by Mack's and see about securing extra protection from the pack."

"Are you sure about that? You aren't exactly on friendly terms with them."

"Yeah, I'm sure. I'm going to need them on my side if the Sterlings come back. As soon as Raeb gets a whiff of her, he'll be on my tail, too. It's not just me I'm thinking about."

"We'll be fine, but if you think the pack's protection is necessary, then I support you."

"I knew you would. See you in an hour."

I ended the call and headed in the direction of Mack's house. If there was anyone who could help me this time around, it was him. He assumed my position when I gave up being Alpha. Over the years, he'd handled some crazy stuff. This would be a cakewalk for him.

Sunrays beamed into my eyes as I made my way down the winding back road. I reached over and punched the glove compartment open in search of my aviators. Should've never taken them off when I got in the car in the first place. Damn blue eyes. They were a constant thorn in my side. It was hard to miss a full-blooded Cherokee with blue eyes. Not to mention they watered like shit whenever the sun was out. With my eyes now shielded by my sunglasses, I returned my focus to the road twisting in front of me.

The pack headquarters was in Townsend. Mack relocated them after my split, saying being so close to the Bear tribe made it difficult during hunting season. It wasn't my deal anymore, but it was a hell of a long drive from Seymour. I spotted the discreet gravel driveway overgrown with weeds on my right and made a sharp turn left into the woods. Every Wolf compound was the same. No road meant no uninvited visitors. The only people who knew where to go were pack members and other shifters following their scent. Humans were oblivious.

Mack was waiting for me beside a beat up Chevy when I halted in front of the large white double-wide mobile home. His long hair hung in a braid over his shoulder, stopping right above a large grease stain streaking across the midsection of his tattered t-shirt. His Alpha tattoo flexed on his bicep as he linked his arms across his chest. Instead of motioning me into the house, he led me to the back where the rest of the pack sat around his barren fire pit.

"So, you're confirming she's here?" Mack asked as he took his position at the head of the group. Since I wasn't a member of the pack, I remained standing outside the circle.

"Yeah, it looks like it."

"Do the others know yet?"

I shook my head negatively. "I don't think so, but it won't be long before they do."

"This legend is going to kill us all," the pack beta Rafe growled. "I say we do her off and be done with it."

My fists clinched as I felt my hackles rise. "No one touches her. Do I make myself clear?" I asked, letting the Supreme Alpha come forward in me. I might've given over my position as Alpha of this pack, but it didn't change the fact I outranked them all.

Rafe cringed as he automatically bared his neck to me in submission. I almost felt guilty. His dad had been my brother before everything went to shit. But, the thought of Star's body being ripped to shreds by sharp wolves' teeth quickly wiped the guilt away. I didn't think about how unnatural it was to be so protective of someone I'd never spoken to. I'd grown accustomed to my jacked up life a long, long time ago.

"Drake is right. Killing her isn't the answer. Our best option is to keep an eye on the others. We'll take shifts watching over her. The Sterlings still want us to pay for what happened to Raphael. I don't trust them to play fair this time around." Mack looked directly at me as he spoke. The others nodded in agreement. Thank God he backed me. He wouldn't be able to touch her because the Supreme Alpha had made a decree, but he could make her life miserable.

"Chances are she doesn't know about what happened before. The family no doubt kept it a secret. We have to make sure she doesn't notice us." I looked around at the people sitting in the circle. All had families and loved ones counting on them. If anyone died during this, their blood would be on me. On the other hand,

Star's death would have the same impact. Only worse. Damn, I was screwed either way.

"We'll start patrolling tomorrow night. Do you know where she lives?" Mack asked.

Unfortunately, I hadn't thought to scan her brain for the information. "I'll have to get it from her tomorrow. I'll send you a message as soon as I know."

Mack nodded before looking at his pack. "We'll take care of her, Drake. You have our word."

When he trained his gold eyes on me, I knew I'd been given the promise of the pack. It goes deeper than anything a simple man could ever guarantee. If one of them broke the promise, they died instantly. My body relaxed knowing I didn't have to worry about them turning on me later when things got bad, which they would. Nothing about Star seemed easy.

I shook Mack's hand and excused myself to head back to my place. Star invaded every space in my mind as I drove. Those unwavering green eyes and the way she looked in all her black clothes. She'd aimed at making herself invisible, but everything about her stood out to me. Might sound lame, but it was like she was a lighthouse and I was the tired, relieved ship lost at sea. She wasn't racked and stacked like a pinup model, which suited me fine. I preferred her lean body, because it was hers. I wondered if she played any sports at her old school.

Everything about her was proportional to her tiny frame. She couldn't be more than five-three, if that. She brought out every protective instinct in me. I wanted to pull her into my arms and shield her from whatever could go wrong in the weeks and months ahead. She looked like she already had enough going on in her life to be worried about the shit I was about to dump into her lap.

I could already hear the others talking when I pulled into the cave and parked my Jeep. Grabbing the jar of peanut butter, I made my way toward the group. It sounded like Rake and Stella were going at it again. Some things never changed.

I squeezed my shoulders through the small mouth of the cave

and made my way through the tunnel to where they were all gathered around a few battery-operated lanterns. As soon as they sensed me, all talking ceased. I looked over at the corner where Bugsey sat with her knees pulled up to her chest, nervously surveying the others. I smiled at her as I tossed her the jar. She clutched it to her chest as a huge smile spread across her face. Before I could take another step, she had the lid off and was spooning the thick spread out with her fingers.

"Wh-what's going on?" Sly asked from his perch in the other corner. My eyes watered the instant his odor reached my nose. It reminded me of rotting garbage and parmesan cheese. Damn, it was stronger than usual, though. Something must've freaked him out today.

I looked over where Rake and Stella glared at each other. Their thoughts were so loud even people who couldn't read minds could hear them.

Idiot thinks coyotes are the superior nocturnal creatures. Raccoons are far better with their gripping capabilities and their ability to reach high places. All coyotes are good for is that creepy whooping sound they made. Mangy mutt. Obviously Stella was pissed at Rake over the same issue they fought about all the time.

Why does she tick me off and make me want to kiss her all at the same time? Whoa! So Rake had a thing for Stella? Looking at both my friends, I couldn't help but wonder what would happen if she ever knew he liked her. She'd probably claw his eyes out.

Stella was all of four-eleven with short silver and black streaked hair. Dark shadows circled her dirt brown eyes, and her little nose twitched the longer she stewed on something. She looked so seemingly innocent, but anyone who'd ever provoked her learned just how deep her claws went.

Rake stalked over to an old metal chair and threw himself into it. His short red hair stuck up in all directions, and his sharp green eyes scanned the room as he fought to control himself. Nothing about him was soft. From his high cheekbones to his long, pointed nose, he looked menacing. Most of us knew he was harmless, but to anyone who crossed him, he was as inviting as the death angel.

I glanced over at Meliena who was playing with the tip of her thick, long braid. The black strands sifted through her fingers as she stared mindlessly into the light. I read her thoughts and realized she was thinking about her husband, John. Every time I saw his face in her mind, guilt twisted in my gut. I doubted I'd ever forgive myself for his death. He'd died because of my beef with the Sterlings. Another victim of this damn legend. Not this time around. Star wasn't going to cause the same wreckage Helena did if I could help it.

"D-Drake? Wh-what's g-going on?" Sly reiterated his question, bringing me back to the present.

"Helena's descendant is in the area." I sighed as I yanked my fingers through my hair, pulling the hair tie out in the process.

"That's bad," Bugsey said as she clutched her precious peanut butter closer to her like a newborn baby.

"Yeah, it's bad. Her name is Star. I've already talked to Mack. He's given me a pack promise they'll help us keep her safe. What we need to focus on now is how to keep history from repeating itself. Either she'll pick one of us and stops the curse, or she won't pick any of us and we could all turn on each other. Worst case scenario, she makes a decision that puts an end to the Guardians forever."

The hierarchy of the Guardians went like this: Destiny, Supreme Alphas, Alphas, Soldiers, and Supporters. Only those with the mark of the Supreme could speak directly to Destiny. And, as of two years ago, I was the only one left. Since no Supreme Alpha had mated and produced an heir in over two hundred years, it all rested on my shoulders to reproduce or the Supreme Alpha line ended with me. No Supreme Alpha, no communication between Destiny and the Guardians. Exhibit A of why Fate wanted me dead.

"What do you mean?" Stella stopped her internal fuming long enough to ask.

"If Star is destined to be with me, and she picks someone else, it's over for *The Guardians*."

Meliena scowled as she looked up at me.

Do you really think she has that much power over us, Drake?

I shrugged as I started to pace. *I don't know. It's been a few centuries since I've had to worry about this.*

"D-do you th-think wh-we'll b-be able to f-fight if i-it c-comes d-down t-to i-it?" Sly stuttered all over himself as he began to fidget. I prayed he kept himself under control. If he sprayed, we'd all be dead...literally.

"With the pack on our side, we can." I answered with a confidence I didn't really feel.

I looked around at the gang. Each had a problem keeping him or her from functioning unsuspected in society.

Rake, the Coyote shifter, was a kleptomaniac and physically couldn't tell the truth if he tried.

Stella, the Raccoon shifter, had a non-existent fuse and was so severely OCD about germs she made herself physically sick worrying about whether the doorknob was washed or if her food had been rinsed properly.

Sly, the Skunk shifter, had an extreme stuttering problem caused by his fear of everything that existed, which caused him to spray *all the time*.

Bugsey, the Squirrel shifter, was a nut hoarder. Her entire kitchen was stocked with bags of nuts, hazelnut spread, and peanut butter. Whenever she felt her stash was in jeopardy, she went postal and bit the intruder. After the fifth time she'd taken a hunk out of the mailman because she thought he'd find her mound of pistachios in the garage, I decided it was best to keep her with us where we could monitor her. I'd had to pay the postal worker a hefty sum to keep him quiet.

Meliena and I were Wolf shifters. Both of us had disassociated from our packs in favor of being loners. I promised John I'd take care of her, but more often than not she was the one who took care of me.

We were our own colony of misfits.

"Where are your crutches?" Stella asked; the first to point out their absence.

"The strength's back in my legs. I think it has something to do with Star coming into town." Which might or might not be a clue that she was my destined mate. It all depended on whether it was an act of Destiny or Fate.

"What kind of name is *Star*?" Bugsey crinkled her nose before she sucked the peanut butter off her fingers.

"Her name," I shrugged. Did it really matter?

"So, what's the plan, boss?" Rake asked as he stretched his legs out.

"I was hoping we could come up with something together."

I glanced over at Meliena and saw the wheels turning in her head. "You've gotta play for keeps this time, Drake. That's all there is to it."

That's what I'd been afraid of. Could I really do this and hold my heart intact? Did I fight to the death, or did I remove myself when the pressure became too much for Star?

"I don't know, Liena. It's not a board game where the end result is *winning* her heart. If she is destined to be with one of us, it doesn't matter what the others try to do."

"I know. It's just a figure of speech. If you say the pull with her is stronger than it was with Helena, then you have a good chance of being the victor this time. You can't think of any other possibilities. She either chooses you or she chooses no one."

This was going to be much harder the second time around. I could already feel it. I paced the length of our cave, wondering if I had what it took to be Star's all in a way Helena never allowed me to be. I still had a hard time accepting Helena hadn't been my destined.

If I'd been wrong with her, what were the chances of my being wrong again with Star?

3

Star

THERE ARE THREE DIFFERENT TYPES OF DAYS. TYPE ONE: THE rainy, miserable day that makes you want to stay inside where it's dry. Type Two: the sunny day that emanates so much perkiness you stay inside because you don't want it to consume you. Type Three: the best in my opinion, the slightly overcast day with brooding clouds and moaning wind where dark souls seem at home. Today was a Type Three day. I sat on a fallen log at the edge of our property, enjoying the feel of the wind teasing its long fingers through my hair.

Breathing grew harder. My eyes burned with tears I refused to shed as I looked down at the thin razor blade in my hand. My friend India said cutting was a way to let out the pain, to focus on something other than the hopelessness consuming my heart on a daily basis. At the time, I thought she was crazy. Had even contemplated reporting her to the guidance counselor. But now? Yeah, I got it.

Today was Clint's favorite type of day, too.

And it was also supposed to be our three-year anniversary.

My hand shook as I studied the blade, wondering if it would really be enough to get rid of his memory.

I lifted my head and squinted as I stared out at the open field behind our house. The wind whipped my hair into my face and in my mouth. I felt some of the strands go up my nose and just left it there. It reminded me of my existence. An existence I despised.

Whenever we were about to have a big storm, Clint would drive us out onto his parents' property and park his old beat-up truck under a large tree overlooking the pecan groves his father owned. We'd climb into the flatbed and snuggle up on a blanket, content to watch the wind rattle the rows and rows of trees. Well, to be more accurate. I'd stare out at the fields while Clint buried his face in my neck. It was an obsession of his.

Just before he'd roll us so that I was beneath him, looking up into his smirking sea green eyes, he'd whisper into my ear, "Whenever we're apart, just look out at the field, and you'll find me."

It was so corny, but a well-aimed missile that worked at sending me into a shivering, hormone-driven mess. He knew I was a sucker for the Catherine and Heathcliff relationship in *Wuthering Heights*, and was always looking for ways to recreate that for us. He was good about that, especially if he thought he would get lucky, which happened nine times out of ten.

At the moment, I could hear his voice clearly. It was lower, deeper than normal; like it'd been the first time he told me he loved me.

Over the howling of the wind, I heard his soft words. "I love you."

God, I'd been so scared and excited the first time he'd said those words.

Clint's older brother Marc worked at the theater complex, and was able to sneak us into an R-rated movie Clint had been dying to see. It was one of those horror slasher movies that basically made you scared to live. Clint loved how I spent the majority of the time with my face buried in his shoulder, but I ended up needing to leave because my stomach couldn't handle all the blood and gore. We snuck back out and sat in his brother's 1979 VW van called the *Shag Shack* to talk until his parents picked us up.

"You're such a chicken," he teased me, poking the spot under my ribs, sending me into the floor with a squeal.

"I can't help it. They were mutilating each other. I thought I was going to hurl." I turned up my nose.

I eyed him with unease, afraid he was going to tickle me again before I could get back up in the seat. He held his hands out in surrender, allowing me to slide next to him on the bench. Our thighs brushed, and I felt the familiar jolt I got whenever we held hands. It started at my feet, went up to my hair and then landed right in the pit of my stomach. I knew what it was – desire. We learned about it in wellness class. By the way he suddenly tensed up, I knew he was feeling the same thing.

He shifted slightly so our knees were touching instead of our thighs. As if that made it any easier. I looked into his beautiful sea green eyes and knew it was the moment I had been waiting for: he was finally going to kiss me, and it would be my first kiss ever. Those radiant eyes moved to my lips and my stomach began to spasm like chipmunks hyped on caffeine were using it as a bouncy house. I had the fleeting fear I was going to throw up on him, but then he took my hand into his and squeezed it, bringing my focus back to us.

He awkwardly lowered his face to mine, a clear indication he was new at it too. I could scarcely breathe because when I did, I drank in his air and it took mine away. Our noses bumped and we chuckled, but he was determined. Finally, our lips met. First, I was disappointed. His lips were dry and the only thing I could think was that he shouldn't have had his mom's garlic bread before we left. Then I was mortified because I ate the bread too and knew he must be thinking the same thing. He must've sensed my hesitation because he pulled away.

"What? Was I not good enough?" he asked. I saw the hurt in

his eyes and I knew I had to act fast or the night would be ruined, not to mention the memory of our first kiss.

"No, just nerves," I said and dove back in.

This time, I didn't know what happened, but suddenly my heart went into my toes and I was shaking from the intensity of it. It was short. Too short. He pulled away and flashed me with a proud smile, and my heart melted under its intensity.

We kissed again, and I felt his tongue push against my lips. At first I didn't know what to do, but then I slightly parted my lips and our tongues met in a wet, sloppy dance that made me crumble against his chest. My toes curled, and I clung to him as if I'd drown if I let go. He let out a groan, and I was blissfully lost.

When he finally decided we needed air, he backed away and rested his head on my forehead like I'd seen couples do in the movies. Then, he placed a kiss on my neck, just below my ear and whispered, "I love you."

I didn't say it back. I couldn't because I was so overwhelmed. We hadn't been dating for three months yet. How could he be so sure what he was feeling was love? God, how could I be sure it was love? It could just be heartburn from the lasagna we'd had for dinner. Thankfully, instead of getting mad, he tugged the collar of my shirt down and began sucking on the base of my neck. My eyes rolled back as I let out a happy sigh, and I accidentally slammed my head on the window.

We both laughed as he pulled me onto his lap so that I straddled him.

Something hard pressed against the place that seemed to be on fire between my legs. My face flushed hot at the knowledge that I'd caused him to respond *that way,* and his face went pink. Neither of us addressed it, but instead I clutched onto the front of his shirt and kissed him with all the emotions I felt but for some reason couldn't voice.

God, that night had changed everything. I'd known then Clint was my forever.

But I'd been wrong.

I felt something hot and sticky on my hand, bringing me back to the present. Glancing down, I saw a thin line of blood flowing from the incision, the blade still slightly embedded in my skin. It didn't matter when I'd done it. All I could focus on was the release. The boiling pain in my chest moved to my wrist, flowed out onto the ground in a small stream, and it felt good. But with the relief came an immeasurable amount of guilt. God, what had I done?

A dog howling in the field broke into my thoughts, bringing me back to reality. If my parents saw this, they'd have me admitted.

I jumped to my feet and hurried inside to the bathroom where I doctored myself up. Once I was positive all evidence of my cutting was gone, I went into the living room where I listened to Dad talk about his job.

The wound on my arm throbbed like the telltale heart, and I worried my parents would be able to see the bandage through the thick black hoodie I wore.

If they did, neither said a word.

4

Drake

I COULDN'T BELIEVE SHE'D GONE THROUGH WITH IT. NO amount of prayer and telepathic messaging had worked. When the blade sliced through her flesh, I felt it down to my core.

It'd hurt like hell to feel her love for another guy. To have to watch the memories play out in her mind. The edges of the recollections had been pink. A sign she was choosing to remember the good instead of focusing on the bad, indicating the relationship hadn't been a healthy one.

Still, as much as it sucked to have to sit through that, it didn't hold a candle to the knife in the gut I got when she cut herself. It'd taken all I had not to burst through the tree line and lick away the blood before a single drop fell on the ground.

A tortured howl ripped from deep within my chest. Star's eyes flew up in my direction, and I froze. There for a moment, I was positive she looked right at me. But, her mind was only focused on getting rid of the evidence as she stumbled into the house.

Stella needed to take over so I could do some work around the house, but I continued to pace along the edge of the woods, letting Star's emotions wash over me.

Guilt was the most overpowering, but misery was also a strong contender. Her parents seemed oblivious to her cry for help, talking and acting like nothing was wrong with their only child. Her heart rate finally regulated, and she was no longer thinking about that guy. Just about the wound on her arm.

I relaxed when she excused herself to her room and turned on her iPod. Arctic Monkeys' "Fluorescent Adolescent" began playing as she stretched out on her bed, staring up at nothing.

I heard a twig snap, and my head turned, gauging the distance.

One mile.

A quick sniff at the air identified warm blood and cinnamon. Definitely not Stella.

Meliena.

When she appeared beside me, I waited as she released the dead rabbit from her mouth. It landed at me feet with a soft thud. She briefly bowed her head in submission before looking me in the eyes.

Stella sends her apologies. She had a work emergency.

Thanks. What's with the food?

I doubt you've eaten anything.

Always the one to look after me. Even when I'd failed her.

Thanks.

Someone has to make sure you're ready for battle.

She sat quietly while I ate, which was unusual for her. Out of the corner of my eye, I saw her silver tail thumping impatiently. Out of respect, I left her thoughts to herself. She'd talk in her own time.

As soon as I finished my last bite, she finally spat out what was bothering her.

I heard some talk on campus that might interest you.

I did a quick check on Star to make sure she was still in her room. The song had changed, and now "The Ice is Getting Thinner" by Death Cab Cutie was on. Her steady breathing was an indicator she'd fallen asleep.

Tell me. I commanded.

There is this new club called the Purists *on campus. They like to call themselves hipsters, but I got a trail on their thoughts. I think they're a new chapter of* Zealots. She shifted uneasily, preparing herself for my outrage.

Shit. I thought they died out back at Salem.

I began to pace. If the Zealots were back, things were about to go from bad to worse.

They're having a hunt this weekend. The words "mutants" and "mutts" were dropped on several occasions. They even have a list of people they plan on capturing. Hesitation lined her words. There was more.

Drake, your name is on the list.

That stopped me in my tracks.

How the hell am I on the list?

Meliena whimpered at my raised voice as her snout lowered to the ground.

There's more. She whined as I towered above her.

Spit it out, Liena! I commanded.

Star's on there, too.

A growl ripped from my chest as I resumed my pacing.

How the hell did a bunch of college pricks get Star's name? I demanded. If I found out one of my own leaked the information, someone was going to die tonight.

The leader of the group goes to your high school. Meliena answered from her lowered position.

Did you get a name? I need a name, damn it!

I loomed over her head, ready to go for the jugular if she answered the wrong way.

No one would even think it. I think they're screening their thoughts.

Damn it, this wasn't good. With Star in Seymour, it was about to be a shifter reunion. The Zealots were a sick, twisted group of fanatics who made it their sole purpose to rid the world of anything unnatural in the name of Christianity, but they weren't Christians. They were monsters. Destiny had silenced them once, but apparently someone had resurrected the old, tyrannical sect. Star's presence was leading the shifters right to their deaths if we didn't do something about it.

It looks like the Falcons are the least of our worries. Meliena muttered as I finally backed down and let her rise.

I turned to watch the light in Star's room flip off. How was I going to keep her safe without her knowing she was in danger? It was going to take all my abilities and breaking all the rules, but failing wasn't an option this time.

I was going to need help, and there was only one person I could ask.

Hopefully she would hear my case and see it worth pursuing.

We're not going to make it out alive, are we? Meliena's voice didn't waver. She was already accepting defeat when the battle hadn't even started.

As long as we stay on the side of good, we'll make it.

It was a partial truth, but even I had a hard time believing it.

I sent up a call to Destiny, knowing she heard. If she decided to give me the time to explain, we had a chance of surviving. Otherwise, this could be the end...for all of us.

﷽ 5 ﷽

﷽

Star

I FELT LIKE THE HAMSTER ON AN EXERCISE WHEEL. NO MATTER how hard I ran, I made zero progress. I just wanted it to stop and break down or something. No, I didn't want to die. I just needed a change, one I actually *wanted* for once.

I hadn't had the urge to cut since the day in the field. To be honest, I wasn't sure why I'd done it in the first place. Yeah, it felt good for the moment, but the truth was Clint's death couldn't be eradicated by my bloodshed. I had to accept that, and he would've killed me if he were alive to see me do it.

So, I threw the razors away, and promised him and myself I would find another way to cope, if that was even possible. To cope, that is.

School was what it was. I went, tried to avoid people, and yet they constantly followed me. I didn't understand it. I never responded to their questions, nor did I contribute to their conversations, yet they always included me as if I had. After a week, I thought I was going to go postal on them.

"Hey Star, we're all going to the basket ball game tonight. Are you game?" Giles asked and laughed at his own joke as we all headed toward the parking lot after school.

"I've got a thing," I shrugged, not liking eight eyes on me.

"What kind of thing?" Onyx asked. The suspicious look she gave me was unnerving.

I didn't answer. Not because it was my usual MO to ignore questions, but because I was terrible at lying on my feet. I inherited that from Mom.

"She is taking lessons with me," A deep voice behind me answer. I turned to see Drake leaning forward on his crutches. I didn't realize he was as tall as he was. He had to be at least six feet if not more. For a guy supposedly on crutches, he moved silently. I hadn't heard him come up on us.

"Oh, well, have fun," Wayley smirked and nudged Onyx as they all walked away, Giles and Chris reluctantly sizing Drake up as they followed.

"Thanks, but you didn't have to do that," I muttered and turned to walk away without looking at him.

"I didn't do anything. Mr. Thomas told me to try to teach you some basic music principles." I looked up in shock, not sure how to respond, only to find his face mere inches from my ear. "You missed your cue all week."

He actually smirked at me! It made him look almost devilish. His eyes twinkled like he had something up his sleeve. I definitely didn't like how I had the insane urge to giggle. Giggle!

"I've gotta go." I tried to brush passed him.

"What are you afraid of?" He was still hovering. I was walking at a power-walk speed. How was he keeping up?

I didn't answer him. When I made it to the front door, he was still there. A frustrated growl rumbled in my chest. I had to do something or he would follow me to Mom's car like a stray dog that decided to adopt me. Mom would never let me hear the end of it. As I turned to say something sarcastic to get him to go away, I realized he could be my get-out-of-jail pass for the night. If I stayed later for the lesson, I'd be able to avoid my parents' constant stares.

"What'd you have in mind?"

When he gave me a smug smile, I noticed he had a slight dimple in his left cheek. His black hair hung freely around his face and his bangs were slightly drooping over his left eye. My fingers ached to brush the hair out of his face. Okay, so I wanted to see if his hair was as soft as it looked.

What was wrong with me?

"Follow me," he crooked a lean finger, and I did as I was told. There was something mesmerizing about him. I guess Mom saw us because out of the corner of my eye I caught her waving at me before driving away. My cell buzzed in my pocket, and I pulled it out. It was her, of course.

"I've got practice," I muttered, not wanting Drake to hear me.

"Can you get a ride from him? I promised your dad I would have dinner ready when he got home."

"Sure," I said before ending the call. No way would I ask him for a ride.

I realized we were going in the direction of the football field instead of the band room. I should've called him on it, but I didn't have enough energy to care. Drake dominated the hallway. Even slumped over on his crutches, people moved out of the way as he walked by them. I couldn't contain the bubble of giddiness that swarmed my system at the possibility people associated me with him.

He led me over to one of the baseball dugouts to the left of the football field. I watched in shock as he leapt up onto the top of the dugout and turned, extending a hand out to me. It was about a six foot jump.

"What the heck?" I sputtered.

"Just take my hand," he sighed, and I looked at said appendage extended out to me.

"You're on crutches. How did you do that?"

"Just grab my hand." Did he just snarl at me?

I had two options. I could take it and spend the afternoon on top of the dugout with this boy who completely mystified and unnerved me; or I could walk away and face my parents. I took my chances and grabbed his hand. He lifted me into the air as if I weighed as much as a small cat, and my feet landed with a loud clang on the metal roof.

"Is this where you bring all the girls?" I asked and immediately wished I could take it back. I didn't want him to think I cared. I did, dang it! Why?

"Sit," he instructed, and I plopped down onto the cool metal like a dog obeying her master. I watched him slowly sit and tuck his legs under him. His eyes briefly scanned over the angry scab on my wrist. If he recognized it for what it was, he didn't say anything. Instead, he focused his attention on making sure his crutches were secure.

"Where is the triangle?" As soon as I asked it, I felt like smacking myself. For the first time since Clint's death, I was starting to actually want to engage in human conversation. It was all wrong. Drake was getting under my skin, and I didn't like it one bit.

Or did I?

What was wrong with me?

"You're sitting on it," he answered as he pulled out a piece of paper from his back pocket. I recognized it as the page they always put in front of me when we started playing in band. There were lines on it and black little characters, but I had no idea what any of it meant.

"You don't have to know any notes for this instrument. It's all about knowing when to make your *ding*," he said.

"So, when's that?"

"Do you see these black bars that look like someone used a black highlighter in the middle of the lines with numbers over them? Those represent measures of rest or the amount of time you don't play. Do you see the two numbers on top of each other at the beginning of those five bar lines?"

"You mean the four over the four?"

"Yeah, that indicates how many beats are in a measure and what note gets the beat. All you need to know is how many beats are in a measure which is the top number."

"Four? What is a measure?"

"Yes, four, and I'm getting to that. A measure is like a frame of time. Count to four and you have a measure. Does that make sense?"

"Getting there," I nodded. In truth, I was so lost. I just prayed something intelligent came out of my mouth so I didn't sound like a total doof to him.

"Okay, in the beginning, you have how many measures of rest before you *ding*?"

I looked at the number over the first bar. "Thirty-two."

"That means you'll count to four thirty-two times. The way you do that is by counting in time with the tempo Mr. Thomas gives you."

"What?" The guy had just left simple-Star kingdom and gone into some alien land. "You know when he says, 'one-two-one-two ready play' and then everyone starts playing? That is him giving you the tempo. How fast he says it and how quickly his arms move are how you know what the tempo or beat is."

"That's where we have a problem. I have no rhythm."

"Just trust me."

It wasn't his fault. He didn't know he was asking the impossible from me.

He spent the next hour trying to teach me how to follow the beat given to me. I never really caught on. The truth was I didn't want to. I was the director of my own life. Also, I was way too distracted by those blue eyes and lean fingers of his. Every time our eyes made a connection, my heart did an Irish jig, and my stomach stirred up the butterflies. It amazed me how calm he was while I was battling with myself over the need to flee and the need to kiss him like crazy.

"I think more sessions are needed," Drake chuckled.

"You know what? This whole thing is stupid. I didn't even want to be in band in the first place," I huffed and started for the edge of the dugout. I wasn't sure how I was going to get off the thing, but I was determined to get away from him as quickly as possible. I might have been projecting my hormonal frustration onto him, but there was only so much a girl could take before she cracked.

"You're going to get yourself killed," he muttered and tossed his crutches onto the ground before jumping down himself. Like nothing out of the ordinary had happened, he turned to reach for me. Again, I was astounded. Why did he use crutches if he didn't even need them?

I wanted to avoid him but fear griped my stomach as I studied how far I was from the ground.

"Are you sure about this? I don't want to hurt you." I bit my lip in indecision.

"Star, I'll be fine. Come on." I saw irritation flitter across his handsome face.

Finally, I jumped into his arms before I gave myself any more time to think. His hands stayed on my waist only long enough to steady me; then he dropped them as if touching me burned him. He turned to retrieve his crutches and prepared himself before leading me away from the field.

"Thanks," I mumbled and slung my bag over my shoulder and began to walk away."My car is in the other direction," he pointed to the back parking lot, the opposite direction of where I was headed.

Rather than trying to come up with some reason why I didn't want to ride with him, I chose to act like I didn't hear and continued walking. Before I could really fathom what was happening, his strong hand clasped over my wrist, and I was spun around in a complete one-eighty. My nose broke my fall against his unwavering chest. I could taste the metal in my mouth before something warm start dancing down my face.

"Ow," was all I managed to say. Tears stung my eyes, and I was positive I broke something, or at least fractured it.

"I'm sorry," I heard him say and something made of cloth was on my face and pinching my nose.

"OW!" I screeched at the pressure.

"Hold still," he spoke calmly.

The pain began to subside a little, but I could still feel the blood coming down. It was revolting, and I knew I must look like a slaughtered victim from a bad horror movie.

"What was that for?" I asked him once my eyes cleared enough to see him.

It was then I realized the cloth on my nose was his shirt. I suddenly felt very awkward. What were people going to think when they saw me standing with my face buried in his shirt while he held me wearing only shoes and jeans? I didn't care if he looked lean and fit standing there with a concerned frown on his face. All I cared about was getting away, but not without an explanation. Besides, what made him take his shirt off? Didn't he have anything else he could've offered?

"I think I overcompensated for your velocity," he said.

"What?"

"You were walking fast, and I tugged a little too hard."

"I know, but why did you *tug*?"

"I've never met anyone as stubborn as you. Your mom wanted me to give you a ride and that's what I'm doing."

I stared at him as if he'd grown an extra head. "How do you know what my mom said? I was the one talking to her on the phone."

"Oh, um," he grew flustered, the way a guy gets when he isn't sure how to tell a girl the truth after she asked him if her dress made her look fat. He ran his hand through his hair before shoving his fists into the front pockets of his jeans in a defensive maneuver. "I overheard her on the phone."

"No, you couldn't have. You were at least a good four or five feet *in front* of me in the hall."

"Come on, forget about the call. Let's just get you home before you drain out your life's blood supply through your nose," he growled.

I was beginning to feel faint and decided that, despite my better judgment I would follow him rather than take my chances of passing out in a ditch for the roadside cleaners to find in the morning. Dying from a loss of blood on the side of a small country road was not how I imagined leaving this world.

He led me to the silver Jeep. The cover was thankfully in place. Maybe no one would see us drive off together.

Like a perfect gentleman, Drake opened the door and helped me in. I mumbled a "thanks" even though his chivalry was annoying. When he started the Jeep, loud music blared over the speakers. If my hands weren't already occupied in trying to keep my nose from bleeding all over his nice leather seats, I would've covered my ears. I settled for a jolt.

"Put your seatbelt on," he instructed and leaned across me to yank the belt down over my chest and snapped it into the buckle. "And keep the shirt on your nose."

"Uh, thanks?"

"Keep your head tilted back. Pinch as hard as you can tolerate to try to stop the blood flow. You're parents will kill me if I bring you home looking like an extra in a horror movie."

"You should've just let me go."

"You really never let up do you?" I heard him mutter under his breath.

Rather than responding to his comment, I stared out the window while trying to decipher what group he was listening to. It sounded like a cross between punk, rock, and Native American. Strange yet cool.

"It's a group from the Reservation."

"Huh?" I turned to look at him.

"The music."

"What Reservation?"

"Cherokee."

"You're into that kind of stuff? That's cool."

"Sort of. I have family there."

"Really? I thought Native Americans had long hair. I mean, yours is longer than most guys' but, I mean, it's just not as long as I thought Native Americans kept it." God, I was fumbling it!

"It depends how you were brought up. Some of us don't follow ritual." It was a short retort, but I felt the heat in his words. Somehow I'd said something wrong. I thought I was merely making an observation. He did have longer hair than most guys, but where his hair stopped just above his shoulders, most Native American men I'd seen had hair ranging in lengths anywhere between a few inches past their shoulders to a few inches above their waists.

"What're they singing about?" I decided to change the subject a little.

"It's an old tribal legend. Some believe we came from the black Bear that lives in the Smoky Mountains, others the Wolf from further north. The Bears once were friends with the Wolves, but then something happened to destroy that bond. Some say it was over this one beautiful woman who came into the village. The Bear chief and the Alpha Wolf thought she was beautiful and fell in love with her instantly, but she wouldn't pick one. They tried to destroy each other fighting over her. This song tells the Bear's story. How much he loved the girl. How she broke his heart."

"Bears?"

"Yeah, crazy, right?" he forced out a chuckle. Something in his ice blue eyes told me he believed in the legend. I pressed my lips together to prevent myself from saying anything else I'd regret later. As long as he was driving me, I wasn't going to provoke him. My free hand clutched the handle bar at my side. My vision blurred, and I started to chill. When had he turned the A/C to the "meat locker" setting?

He was asking me about something or saying something. I

wasn't sure. The only thing I was positive about was that I was seeing stars.

I'm not really sure what happened next. One minute I was forcing myself to stare at a stop sign to regain focus and the next I was looking up into blue eyes filled with deep concern. The face they belonged to was only inches away from mine. Nice.

"Star, are you okay?" the deep voice rumbled.

"Huh?" I was clearly dazed. What happened?

"I think she's going to be fine. Probably just weak from the loss of blood." It was the voice again. I was almost certain it belonged to the face I was staring at.

"Star is known for being a klutz from time to time."

I knew that high voice. Mom. Hearing her words brought me back to reality, and I became acutely aware of how dangerously close I was to Drake's face. I tried to move, but I felt like someone had strapped me down to the ground. Said straps being Drake's immovable arms. It was like being dead-bolted to an iron beam.

"Can I sit up?" I asked him.

As if my words somehow broke the spell, Drake leapt back onto his heels, and I was able to sit up. I looked down at my blood-soaked black t-shirt and winced. Great. It was my favorite one, too.

"Honey, put this on your nose. You really ought to be more careful where you go," Mom scolded.

I took the bag of frozen peas she held out to me. It stung like holy fire as I pressed it against my nose, a sharp hiss leaking through my teeth at the contact.

"It's probably broken, but there's not much you can do," my dad was saying.

I looked over at Drake and watched as an unreadable expression crossed over his face. I was usually good at reading people but he masked his emotions, reining them in like a guard outside Westminster Abbey.

"Would you like to stay for dinner?" It came from Mom. She had that lilt in her voice she got when she was up to something.

"He's got homework to do," I answered for him before slowly trying to stand.

I had almost succeeded in my mission when my knees buckled and I lurched forward. Of course Drake was there to catch me. I wished he'd just let me fall. His strong, reassuring arms wrapped around my waist were doing funny things to my brain.

"Thanks, but Star is right. Got a chem test tomorrow that I haven't started studying for," he shrugged as he righted me.

"Well, thanks for bringing her home." She was disappointed. Good.

Dad wrapped his arm around my shoulders and steered me toward the house. I could hear Drake saying something but didn't try to make out the words. Once I was in my room, I collapsed on my mattress and went to sleep immediately. Mom woke me up every hour but eventually she just let me sleep. I should've been able to escape from the pain but it morphed into the pain that came from watching Clint die over and over in my dreams. I was never going to escape this torture, was I?

6

⊙⊛⊙

Drake

SHE'D LOST HER FIRST LOVE.

She blamed herself for his death and had convinced herself she didn't have the right to enjoy life...or love.

Damn it! It explained the cutting, the depression, the determination not to feel the attraction between us.

My fist slammed into the punching bag I'd spent the last hour punishing. I watched it fly off its hinges and explode against the concrete wall.

I could handle competing with one of the Sterlings or Raeb, but I couldn't fight a ghost. She'd memorialized him. If they'd had a soul-mate bond, none of us stood a chance. We'd all end up killing each other. But the pink tint to her memories gave me hope. Hopefully soon, all the dark stuff in their relationship would surface...if there was dark stuff.

I punched my fist into the wall. Seeing the concrete crack did nothing to alleviate the rage inside me.

She'd finally loosened up a little with me. Then I pissed her off. That hadn't been so smart. I lost my head when I was around her. Something about her made me want to let down my walls. Not something I was comfortable with.

My phone chirped, cutting through my frustration for at least a moment.

Mack: First night on patrol. So far, no sightings. Keep you posted.

Me: Thanks.

Mack: What are you going to do about the dead boyfriend?

Shit, I knew I couldn't hide it from Mack. I hated the damn wolf telepathy. It was like an old school party line. No secrets ever.

Me: I'll think of something.

Mack: You better.

As if I needed the reminder. I threw my phone across the room and stalked out the barn into the darkness. I needed to run. Breaking all the equipment in my gym wasn't cutting it. I tossed my clothes onto the hood of my Jeep before I lurched forward. The Wolf pushed to the surface and my vision sharpened as I fell onto all fours.

Home

No matter how fast or hard I ran, I couldn't shake her. Those haunting green eyes kept flashing in my mind. What mesmerized me about them was the bridled desire shining in their depths. She wanted me. I could smell it on her. But, she didn't want to want me.

Back on the dugout I'd wanted to kiss her until I made her mine.

The snap of a twig halted me midstride, and I tilted my head as I trained my ear to the sound. The scent of cinnamon tickled my nose and I relaxed.

Why am I not surprised?

A few moments later, Meliena's gray coat came into view. She nudged my side with her head as she sat down on her haunches.

What's wrong, Drake?

I paced in a circle around her. Her tail swished, almost tripping me. I sent her a glare, but she just smirked.

She lost a boyfriend...recently. Her heart's still loyal to him.

Meliena's head bowed and a whimper escaped. John flashed into my mind and I winced. The years still hadn't dulled his memory for her. If Star loved this Clint guy as much as Meliena loved John...,

I couldn't even think about what that meant for me.

How long ago? Meliena asked.

Not long. Probably a few months ago. Maybe a little longer.

She's grieving, Drake.

You don't think I know that? I shot her a vicious glare. This was going to go to shit fast and we both knew it.

You can't come on too strong or she'll run away.

I growled, letting my hackles rise. *Mind your own business, Liena.*

Meliena nudged me. *You can't give up before you even try.*

I climbed onto a rock and looked up at the half moon. The man in me remembered how good it felt to have her in my arms. She'd smelled like heaven and felt like home. Even better than wolfing out. I'd wanted to stay in the front yard with her forever. It hurt to know I'd caused her pain, even if it was unintentional.

How could she twist me up like this so soon? Unless she was my destined. Damn Fate. Odds were all of us were programmed to think Star was our destined. We'd fight each other to the death when in reality she was destined for someone else.

Give yourself a chance, Drake. You'll surprise yourself.

I turned in time to see Meliena's gray wolf disappear into the night.

Distance. I needed distance. I turned in the direction of the mountains and ran. Something told me I could run all the way to China (if that was even possible), but I'd never be able to outrun Star.

7

Star

"WHAT HAPPENED? YOU LOOK LIKE A RACCOON," GILES SAID AS soon as I sat down at the lunch table.

"Thanks," I muttered.

"Giles! You're such a doof burger." Wayley rolled her eyes. "Anyway, we're all going to the movies tonight. Wanna come? It's that new vampire thriller." Wayley's eyes grew large with glee. I wondered if she was excited about watching vampires drink human blood, or if she was wound up about spending two hours salivating over the lead actor as he strutted around shirtless.

I knew my parents were scrapbooking as soon as dinner was finished. It was Mom's idea. She thought maybe doing family projects would bring me out. Being terrified by blood-drinking vampires sounded like the better alternative.

"Sure," I shrugged.

"Really? You really wanna come?" Wayley stared at me like I'd grown a second head. "Why are you surprised?" I was uncomfortable with her shock.

"Well, usually we invite you and you come up with a reason to back out. This is good," Onyx gave me an encouraging smile.

"You can sit next to me." Giles winked.

"No, she'll be sitting next to me." Chris had the audacity to drape his arm across my shoulders. "Gotta protect her from all that evil."

"I think I'll just sit between Onyx and Wayley," I shrugged his arm off and shoved a strand of hair behind my ear.

The jab didn't daunt him. He flashed me a goofy grin, and I found myself comparing him to Clint. They were built the same. Clint was probably just a few inches taller. Both had ash blonde hair that could be mistaken for white, except Clint had always kept his short. Chris's hair was on the shaggier side, like he rolled out of bed and squirted a little gel in it. Chris's eyes were hazel. Clint's had been the perfect shade of sea green or turquoise, whatever was my choice of description for the day. That was where the comparison stopped. I felt my throat tightening up like I'd swallowed a wad of bread without chewing it good. If I didn't change my thoughts, I was going to have an emotional breakdown in front of total strangers who'd then know the ugly truth of my life.

The hairs on the back of my neck stood at attention as I felt a presence behind me. Without turning I knew it was Drake. But, I turned and looked anyway. Something beyond my control compelled me to him the second he was on my radar. Weird.

"Mind if I sit here?" He pointed to the vacant seat to my left. I didn't have to glance at the others to know they were all staring. I mean, who wouldn't stare at him? No one had the right to be that hot.

To avoid drawing more attention to myself, I nodded. "Sure."

Drake sat down, shoving his crutches under the table before pulling out a brown bag from his backpack. I watched each graceful movement, wondering how he managed to make the most mundane of tasks seem...spectacular. He surprised me by resting his large, warm hand on my thigh and giving it a gentle squeeze. My leg jerked as warmth spread throughout my body.

Ah, that was...yeah, I had no words.

"How's the nose?" He asked low enough only I could hear.

"Fine. I only notice it when I bump it, or when I look in the mirror." I was so proud of myself for sounding cool, because I definitely wasn't feeling it inside.

"I'm sorry you're hurt." He drew circles on my thigh as he spoke, causing my brain to completely shut down. My body shimmered under the mindless ministration, and my eyes dropped to half mass. I might have possibly purred; it felt that good.

One minute I'd been on the verge of tears, the next I was turning to putty at the simple touch of his hand. Amazing.

"So, about tonight. I can pick you up if you want," Wayley offered, finally finding her voice. Or had she been talking before, I just hadn't noticed? Did it even matter?

It took me a few seconds to push past the fog in my brain to come up with a coherent answer.

"Do you know where I live?"

"Yeah, just down the street from me. I saw your family move in."

I nodded but didn't verbally answer. That was all the communication she needed to know I agreed with her plan.

"Okay, I'll be by your house at...wait, why don't we just ride home together? You can hang out at my place until it's time to go."

I shrugged. It beat going home.

"What are you doing tonight?" Drake asked me.

But of course, it was Wayley who answered. "We're going to see *Vampire's Revenge*. You wanna come?" She bounced in her seat like an eager Chihuahua.

I tried not to look like I cared one way or the other when Drake refused to take his eyes off me. But the truth was I really, really wanted him to come with us. Being around him made me uncomfortable. A good type of uncomfortable. The kind that made me feel almost human; something that had been missing in my life since they buried Clint. I felt...complete around Drake.

"Sure, if Star doesn't mind."

All eyes fell on me, and I fought the urge to bury my face in his shoulder. God, I didn't do well with attention.

"I don't mind," I mumbled, and his fingers resumed their seductive dance on my thigh. His pinkie went errant, slipping over my inner thigh, so close to my "no no" zone, and my body went on red alert. Before I could say anything his hand shifted to safer regions.

"Great! This is gonna be so much fun."

Wayley went off on a tangent about a girl named Brittney in her French class, and I was content to drown myself in my lettuce with no dressing. When the bell rang, we all gathered up our crap so the next lunch group could take our places.

I waited on Drake while the others walked on ahead of us.

"I have to take care of some business before the movie or else I'd drive you myself," he said once he had his backpack in place and his crutches supported all his weight.

"It's fine. You don't have to come if it'll cause you problems. Wayley gets carried away like that sometimes." I shrugged as I matched my pace to his.

"Someone has to hold your hand when the blood drinking gets to you." He gave me that smirk. God, I had a love/hate relationship with that sly grin, and I hardly knew him.

I rolled my eyes and shoved my hair out of my face.

"See you tonight." He winked as he turned to go the opposite direction of me.

"What about band?"

"Not going today. Like I said, I've got a thing." He grinned like skipping was no big deal. Even in my dejected state of living, skipping was a big deal.

"A *thing*?" To be honest, my mind went straight to the gutter.

"Yeah," he nodded as if that said it all before hobbling on to wherever it was he was headed. Maybe to deal with his *thing*.

That made me snicker.

I walked to calculus without further incident and busied myself at my desk, getting ready for class.

"Star, why don't I just meet you in the band room after school?" Wayley asked as soon as I had my homework assignment out and stopped fidgeting.

"I don't think you want to brave that place." Giles grimaced as he plopped down into the seat directly behind me.

"What's so terrible about the band room?" Onyx huffed, apparently taking up for her fellow band mates as she took her seat next to him.

"Probably afraid of the monster hiding in the uniform room that smells like stale B.O. and peanuts," I snorted.

Giles tilted his head back as his body shook with laughter. It really wasn't that funny but apparently it was to him and his contagious cackles got everyone else involved.

"You all are strange."

Class was boring and uneventful. By the time the bell rang, I was pretty sure my brain had leaked out into a pool at my feet.

৩৩৩

As promised, Drake wasn't in band. It should've made me happy, but I missed avoiding his stares. Since our practice session yesterday, I couldn't help but want to spend more time with him. He was quiet and possibly moodier than me, but there was something about him that drew me like a magnet to a metal refrigerator. I was two parts excited and one part scared about seeing him tonight. No matter how I tried to put it in my head, somehow my mind twisted the outing into a group date.

Would he sit beside me? Would he try to hold my hand? Would he be upfront about it or do the whole hands-bumping-in-the-popcorn-bucket bit? Ahh, I needed to stop!

True to her word, Wayley met me in the band room as soon as the last bell rang. I allowed her to do all the talking as she drove us to her house. It really was on the same street as mine and looked the same, too: 1950s retro brick with split foyers.

"Before we go inside, I want you to meet my dog." She cut the engine before springing out.

Wayley led me to the backyard where a black lab was barking and loping from one side of the yard to the other, tail wagging eighty miles an hour.

"Star, Prynne, Prynne, Star."

"Prynne? As in Hester Prynne from *The Scarlet Letter?*"

"We were reading the book when my parents brought her home. I first wanted to name her Hester, but Mom thought it might be a little too much ego for one dog, so Prynne it was. I call her Prynney most of the time."

Prynney jumped up and plopped her big, dirty paws on my stomach the moment we stepped through the gate. Inwardly I was begging for someone to get the mutt off me.

"Uh, nice dog," I said awkwardly, trying not to touch her. I hated animals. Too much fur and not enough brains. Sure, they were fine from a distance, but being up close to them was a different story.

"Oh, Prynney, be nice to Star." Wayley was leaning over, trying to pull the dog off me. "I think she likes you."

"Can't say the feeling is mutual."

Wayley only giggled and diverted Prynne's attention with a bright green tennis ball. "Go get it!"

The ball launched into the air and Prynne charged after it, her muscular back legs barely keeping up with her. She grabbed it and returned to drop it at my feet. Wayley laughed and threw it again. While this game continued, I sat down in an iron chair on her patio and stared at the ornate pattern dancing across the matching iron table. My eyes zeroed in on the hole in the center where an umbrella was supposed to be. I felt like that hole, missing something that was normally there. All that was left was the space it'd made.

"Dammit." It was just a whisper, but I felt the frustration I was bottling up inside eek out with the simple word. I was really tired of having to fight emotions all the time. Why couldn't I just move on like everyone else? My heart twisted awkwardly, and I wasn't sure I was ever going to breathe again. Oddly enough, my heart cried out in need...for Drake's arms around me.

"Want to get something to drink? I think my mom made peach tea last night." Wayley's words shook my brain enough to make my lungs function, but they weren't enough to take away the pain.

What the heck was happening to me?

"Peach tea?" The question squeezed out through my constricted lungs.

"You're from Georgia and you haven't had peach tea?"

"Not all of us are into that sort of thing." I was regaining feeling in my arms, and my breathing was back to normal. The throb was now only a dull thud.

"Well, you have to try it. Come on."

We walked into her house, and I immediately realized how wrong I'd been. Our homes may be similar on the outside but the inside of Wayley's looked like something straight from the *Home and Garden* channel. Votive candles twinkled in every corner and the walls radiated with olive green warmth. The den was decked with a large leather sofa and matching chair-and-a-half. The kitchen was completely modern with stainless steel fixtures and granite countertops.

It couldn't be more obvious that we came from two different worlds. Nothing in my house matched because my parents sold everything they had to move here and stopped at various garage sales along the way between Atlanta and Seymour to stock up on the essentials.

"We used to have lavender cookies but it looks like my dad took those."

"Lavender? Is that common around here?"

"Oh no. Dad's a diabetic, so we've experimented with ways to make his favorite foods where he can eat them again."

"Huh." I grunted. Still weird.

She opened the spacious refrigerator and pulled out a glass pitcher filled half-way with tea. I turned away and was content to stare out the window at a massive oak tree blocking my view of the mountains. Its limbs were barren, a stark contrast to the gray sky.

"Drink up."

I looked down at the glass shoved at me and resolved myself to being Wayley's lab rat. I said a silent prayer and took a sip. It wasn't as bad as I thought it'd be. Slightly on the quirky side but still drinkable.

I finished the drink, and she stuck our glasses in the dishwasher before giving me the grand tour. We eventually made it to her room, which was an explosion of bright pink. I felt like running back to my room where there was nothing but unopened boxes and white walls. I couldn't handle all the cheerfulness. Not even back in my pre-Clint days could I have handled this much perkiness in one room. It was candy syrup mixed with artificial food coloring. My tongue recoiled like I'd swallowed a mouthful of hairspray. She plopped herself onto her bed, and I decided to take the magenta pink computer chair. The place even smelled pink.

"So, are you interested in any boys at school?"

I had a feeling that was where her thoughts would go. She was into Chris. I'd gotten the message loud and clear last week when she "accidentally" fell into his lap on her way to her seat at lunch. Frankly, they'd make a cute couple, if she could keep her mouth shut long enough for him to ask her out.

"No."

"What about Drake?"

"Never."

"Hum, I thought you two seemed to be hitting it off, especially since he's coming with us tonight. He practically invited himself."

"He's probably just bored." I shrugged, trying to play it down. Even I knew there was something going on. Guys didn't touch girls' thighs unless they were interested. At least no guy I'd ever known did anyway.

"No, he's into you. Drake Knight doesn't do social events. He's the dark, sexy loner. This is huge."

I shuffled uncomfortably in my seat. "Whatever."

"I'm serious. Once word gets out, you're going to be a legend." Wayley tossed her blonde hair over her shoulder as she rolled onto her back.

"What's his story anyway?" I found myself asking. Onyx had given me her version. I was curious to see if Wayley's was any different. Not that I'd take either girl's word as law where Drake was concerned. Why trust a third party when you could get the truth straight from the source?

"No one really knows. All the girls try to hook up with him, but he never shows any interest. Supposedly, he did a stint in juvie. Only dates college girls. Doesn't have any friends. At least not at school. Tends to stick to himself. I heard he has a bad temper. That he got kicked out of ALC because he beat up a teacher."

"ALC?"

"Alternative Learning Center. It's where the bad kids go after being suspended or expelled one too many times." She shrugged.

"Why would he be transferred to a public school if he beat up a teacher in the alternative school?"

"How would I know?" she flopped back onto her stomach with a smile. "So, would you be okay if I tried to sit by Chris tonight?" She asked, effectively changing the subject.

"Of course. As long as I'm between you and Onyx, I don't care."

"What about Drake?" She frowned.

"Put him beside Giles."

Wayley was satisfied to talk about the latest relationship drama happening within their social group, and I slipped into a mental state of numbness. It was the first time I'd literally felt nothing. If I'd been able to feel, I would have said it was wonderful. Instead, I just stared down at my black converse shoes.

"You know, I bet you would make a great blonde."

"It's red." I fought of the urge to play with my hair now that it was the topic of conversation.

"Deep or light?"

Why the hell did it matter? Still, I answered, "Like cherry coke."

"Why did you go black?"

"Felt like it."

"I thought about going chocolate brown once." She began studying her hair in the full-length mirror mounted on her wall.

"Don't. Guys like blondes." The words flew out my mouth, but I wasn't thinking them through. However, I knew if I wanted to use Wayley as an excuse to get away from my house, I had to somewhat act like a friend. I wasn't sure how long she'd find my "social outcast" behavior endearing.

"Apparently they like black, too."

"No, I'm just a novelty. Once the newness wears off, they'll forget I exist."

Wayley pulled out some fashion magazines and started talking about different styles she should try. I nodded in all the right places but didn't say anything. Finally, she looked down at her watch and declared it was time to go.

The theater was packed by the time we got there. Giles and Chris were loaded down with massive tubs of popcorn and M & Ms. Somehow the seating arrangement ended up being Chris and Giles in the middle with Onyx and Wayley flanking them. I sat on the other side of Wayley with an empty seat on my left reserved for Drake. I blamed my perky seat neighbor for *that* coincidence.

The movie trailers began with no sight of Drake, giving me false hope he was going to be a no-show. Unfortunately, he slid into the vacant seat just as the opening credits started.

"Miss me?" he whispered in my ear.

I snorted.

Out of the corner of my eye I caught Chris leaning forward to glower at us. As much as I wanted to set him straight with the truth-that Drake and I weren't a couple-it was a good thing to have him think something was going on. He needed to carry a torch for someone else. Preferably Wayley.

The main character came onto the screen and Wayley immediately started wiggling beside me.

"Dude's airbrushed. What a dud," Drake whispered, his warm breath rushing over my neck, causing my skin to prickle.

I turned to give him my "shut up before I slap you" face, and then redirected my attention to the screen.

About fifteen minutes into the movie, Drake reached over the armrest dividing us to grab my hand from my lap and tug it into his. He linked our fingers together, squeezing tight when I tried to pull away. To avoid making a scene, I gave in and tried to focus on the movie. Fat load of good that did.

He had a nice hand; large, warm, and lightly calloused. I felt secure...safe. Sometime during the movie, he began playing with my palm, tracing every line, crease, and ridge. When his thumb brushed over my wrist, I squirmed, shocked at the jolt of pleasure that coursed through my veins. My blood started to hum, and I was beginning to feel lightheaded. Who the heck would've thought my wrist would be a hot button?

"So this is what having sex with a corpse looks like," he muttered a while later when the leading roles were doing the horizontal in a crypt. Ew.

"Huh?" I frowned. What the heck was he talking about? The vampire guy was acting very much alive while he ravished the mortal girl. Or was I missing something.

"The actress looks like a dead fish," he snickered.

I tilted my head to the side as I studied her closely. She moaned in all the right places, but otherwise, Drake was right. Her hands stayed lifeless by her side and not once did she move her head. It was a little disturbing to watch, to be honest.

"Shut up and watch the movie," I hissed, glancing around to make sure we weren't drawing attention.

Drake leaned his head down, brushing his lips over my ear as he whispered, "Be honest. You see it, too."

Nerve endings I didn't know I possessed stood at attention at the contact. I swallowed hard as I nodded affirmatively. He chuckled and resumed torturing my over-sensitized hand. Okay, so it wasn't torture. More like heavenly bliss, but his touch shouldn't feel that good. Not so soon after Clint.

I'll be honest and say I didn't catch most of the movie. How could I focus on anything when Drake's fingers were causing little explosions to go off in the lower region of my body every time he clustered his fingers together in the center of my palm and then expanded them out to mesh our hands together before retracting back to the center? It was thrilling and hypnotic, leaving me feeling like a shimmering hot mess. He provided further snarky commentary throughout the entire movie, causing me to snicker at the most inappropriate times. Yet, no one shushed us, so obviously we were keeping the volume down. Thank goodness for small miracles.

Even though I was a little preoccupied, I managed to get the gist of the movie. Immortal, lonely vampire meets mortal girl, they fall in love, but she turns him down when she realizes the only way they can be together is if he turns her into a vampire. Vampire dude tries to kill himself but can't die. The end. Not all that earth-shattering if you asked me.

Put simply, it sucked.

"That was a lame movie. Where was all the killing and the blood-drinking? Or at least an angry mob that comes after him to burn him piece by piece. Anything other than all that mushy-gushy stuff," Chris grumbled as we left the theater, following the masses out to the parking lot.

"I thought what those two had was so precious," Onyx sighed, her eyes glazed over with wonder-lust.

"Too bad the girl turned him down or else we would've at least seen some blood drinking," Giles complained.

"You boys just don't understand romance." Wayley frowned as she slid her arm through the crook of Chris's.

I was with the boys. She should've allowed herself to become a vampire. Of course I knew vampires didn't exist, and that my body would eventually die. But, something had changed inside of me. For the first time since his death, I realized just how much I needed to live and feel alive. I only had this one life. Might as well try to enjoy it. But to live forever on this earth had a certain appeal. Sure, it was messed up, but it was the only earth I'd ever known.

It didn't get rid of the guilt I carried: I was able to live my life while Clint rotted in a shinny box six feet under.

Drake slipped his arm around my shoulder, drawing my attention to the fact he was walking free of crutches. When I looked up at him to ask the obvious, he placed a finger over his lips and winked, nodding at the others. Was he trying to point out to me just how self-involved and clueless these people were? Because, hello, old news. I could've told him that.

"What did you think of the movie?" he asked me.

I shrugged. "It was okay. It would've been better if she'd chosen him in the end. It felt like the writer ran out of time and slapped on a quick ending. It's going to be hard to build a sequel off that."

"Unless a new girl comes who will pick him," Onyx argued.

"True, but with nothing else driving the plot, is it really worth watching? It would be the same movie all over again, just with an alternate ending," I tossed back.

"I'm with Star on this one," Chris piped in.

"Well, good thing the decision isn't up to us," Wayley shrugged. "I'm starving. Let's go get something to eat."

The group decided to go to an all-organic restaurant in Market Square just a block or two over from the theater. I'd never been, but Drake seemed interested so I trusted his judgment. As we crossed the street, Drake held me close to his side, not saying a word.

I couldn't understand why I was allowing him to touch me, let alone hold me like he was trying to shield me from any impending evil. What was even more mindboggling was how empty I felt when he released me to pull my chair out once we were inside and directed to our seats.

The conversation flowed smoothly amongst Onyx, Wayley, Chris, and Giles. Drake and I sat at the end of the table, content to be silent observers. Every now and then I'd catch him staring unashamedly at him. I'd dart my eyes away from his and my cheeks flushed.

While I ate my tofu and cheese sandwich, which was surprisingly really good for tofu, I listened to Chris and Onyx debate over which phone-booth time traveling machine was better, the one in *Dr. Who* or the one in *Bill & Ted's Excellent Adventure*. I wasn't familiar with either, so I just listened.

I noticed Drake didn't eat anything.

"Are you sure you don't want anything? I can give you half my sandwich. It's not like I'll be able to eat this whole thing anyway," I said, holding out half to him.

His silver eyes twinkled as he smiled endearingly at me, which was a little disconcerting. "I'm good, but thanks. I didn't know we were going out afterward so I ate before I came."

I opened my mouth to ask what his plans were for the weekend when his phone rang. Glancing at the screen, he frowned before answering. I tried not to eavesdrop, but there was nothing to hear. After a few non-committal grunts, he ended the call and stuffed his phone back into his pocket.

"Everything alright?" I asked as casually as possible.

"I need to leave. Can I give you a ride home?"

I was about to decline when Wayley piped in, "She'd love that."

Knowing I'd be wasting my breath if I protested, I stood and slipped back into my jacket. Drake tossed enough bills on the table to cover both our meals before guiding me out. I glanced over my shoulder to catch Wayley winking at me before I walked out the door. If I could use magic, I'd so turn her into a bug so I could squash her at that moment.

Drake and I walked briskly to the garage where his Jeep was parked. The wind blew strong and sent frigid tendrils down my collar and numbed my face. He tugged me to his side, shielding me from the brunt of it. By the time we climbed into his SUV, my nose was dripping and my teeth clanked together. Thank God for seat warmers, because I couldn't feel my butt.

Once we were out of the garage, I had to talk. For some reason, I wasn't okay with the silence. A first, I know, but I needed to hear his voice.

"So, um, what did you think about the movie?" I asked, sucking in my bottom lip. Why was it always like this? Jittery, nerve wracking, and comforting all at once?

"Don't do that," he growled when he glanced over at me.

"What?" My eyebrows shot up to my hairline. What the heck had I done?

"Bite your lip like that."

Huh? "Why?"

"Because I can't be responsible for my actions if you keep doing that." The muscle along his jaw line flexed as he gripped the steering wheel tight enough it made a popping sound.

Oh. My. God.

Somewhere deep down inside, curiosity sparked, lighting a promising flame in my heart. I was almost tempted to bite my lip again to see what would happen, but he made the decision for me by answering my previous question as if the exchange hadn't happened. "It would've been better if there was some fighting or bloodshed."

"Yeah, and what was with the pretty boy she randomly picks in the end? The mortal. So not who I would've picked," I laughed nervously.

"She was thinking with her joy stick." Drake smiled mischievously.

It took me a second to catch the meaning before I started laughing. "That's disgusting! Girls don't do that!" I swatted his shoulder.

"Trust me, they do." He challenged me with a raised eyebrow.

"Give me an example," I demanded.

"Wayley."

I frowned, not expecting that. "What about her?"

"She wasn't interested in that guy for his intelligence and sparkling wit, Star. She was imagining him with his pants off and inside her."

"Ugh! That's disgusting. No she wasn't! Not everyone thinks in the gutter like you."

Drake turned to look at me as he stalled at a red light. "Trust me on this, babe."

Oh, but his eyes were hypnotic. I'm pretty sure scientists would find proof that black holes existed in his silver orbs.

A mental reminder of sea green eyes I used to love to stare at once snapped me out of whatever trance I'd been put under.

"What would you do different with the movie?" I brought us back to the original conversation.

A slow grin inched on his face. "I'd have some naked girls."

"You're such a guy." I rolled my eyes.

"That's what you like about me."

His eyes dropped to my lips, which made me involuntarily look at his. They were full and slightly parted. He moved his hand to cup the back of my head as he pulled me closer to him. This was happening. He was going to kiss me, and I was going to let it happen.

Someone's quick panting, probably mine, reverberated throughout the vehicle just before he lowered his head. My breath hitched as his lips brushed softly against my cheek. A horn blared, breaking the spell. Drake released me to focus his attention on the road while I stared blindly out the window.

What the heck just happened?

All too soon, we were in my driveway. I saw my parents' silhouettes in the front window and groaned.

"I forgot to call them after school."

Drake moved to open his door, and I shot my hand out to stop him. "I've got this. Stay inside."

He shrugged my hand off before climbing out of the Jeep. I

watched as he skirted the hood of the SUV and opened my door, panic clawing at my throat. My parents were going to kill him.

"I'm not letting you talk to my parents, Drake," I warned; his safety the most important thing on my mind.

"Who said anything about talking to your parents?" He asked as he reached across my midsection to unbuckle me. I hadn't realized I'd yet to move. Butterflies released in my stomach under his touch.

"Then what are you doing?"

"I'm walking you to the door."

"Huh," I huffed as he wrapped his hands around my waist and hoisted me out of the Jeep and onto my feet as if I weighed nothing.

He linked our fingers, together and led me to the porch. I kept my eyes on the ground, so not ready to face the wrath of my parents.

At the doorstep, he gave me a quick hug and a light kiss on my forehead, making me feel like a little kid. "Tell your parents it was my fault," he whispered into my ear just as the front door swung open.

Mom's angry face was illuminated by the porch light.

"Say goodnight to Drake," she ordered.

"Don't be mad at him. I went to the movies with Wayley. He was just giving me a ride home," I explained.

Did Drake just growl beside me? Because it definitely sounded like an angry wolf or tiger.

"I know. We'll discuss this inside. Goodnight, Drake."

Drake opened his mouth, obviously ready to protest, but then let out a frustrated sigh. "Goodnight, Mrs. Allistar." Drake waited until I was inside before he went back to his Jeep. Even without looking at him, I knew he wasn't happy with the way the night ended.

"Go to your room," was all Dad said as I walked passed him.

I obeyed. Maybe they were so pleased I was out with friends that they would let this one slide. I changed into shorts and a hoodie before washing my face in my bathroom. When I returned to my room, Dad was leaning against the door frame.

"Did you have a good time?"

I studied his face to see if he was being sarcastic. The lack of emotion in his voice almost tricked me into believing he was okay with it all, but judging by his hard, angry eyes, he was definitely being facetious.

"Just saw a vampire movie," I played along.

"Your mother and I are disappointed. We've been trying to reach you all evening, thinking you were dead somewhere. When Wayley's mom called and said you went to the movies and left your stuff at their house, we were first relieved, then furious. The purpose of giving you a cell phone was so you could call us when you made plans. You are only a senior in high school, Elizabeth. When you're out of the house, you can live by your own rules. Until then, it's our rules. You're grounded for three weeks."

"Okay." For me, that wasn't a punishment. I saw the frustration in his eyes and inwardly smiled. If he really wanted to punish me, he would've made me go out every night.

He turned around and walked out of the room without saying another word. I plopped onto my mattress and thought the worst part was over. As I was about to slip into sleep, Mom came barging in and gave me a two-hour lecture about how irresponsible I was and how it wouldn't hurt to start being part of the family again. I listened, but kept silent. When she left, I went to sleep and dreamt of Drake.

I'D ONLY BEEN ASLEEP FOR AN HOUR WHEN THE SOUND OF AN animal's howl woke me. It sounded... sad. I decided to step out onto the back porch and investigate. Stuffing my feet into a pair of old black Crocs, I shuffled quietly through the house and out the back door.

I was a nerd for the moon and its phases. Tonight, a waxing

gibbous moon peeked out from behind the clouds, giving the night sky a natural blue glow. The hoot of an owl sent shivers down my spine. Instead of walking around, I sat down on the porch swing and just listened. The howl came again. I stared at the thick of woods directly behind my house and watched as a dark form shifted. I held my breath, unsure of what it was. Then, the moon came out again, casting a glow on the object.

Standing only fifty feet away from me was the largest wolf I'd ever seen. It was solid black and looked like it could eat a bear for a snack. My brain was shouting for me to run, but I sat motionless watching the wolf inch closer. It stopped about twenty feet away from me, and we stared at each other for a moment. A noise came from inside the house and startled him. I yelped in protest as he darted away.

Take me with you! My heart cried. To be so free without a care in the world. God, I wanted to be that wolf.

"Hey," Dad's voice came from behind me.

"Don't worry, I was just about to go inside," I mumbled and stood to my feet.

"No, sit down. I think you and I need to talk."

I plopped back down and waited for what he had to say. I was tired of all the talks.

"Your mom and I care about you. You know that, right?"

I nodded.

"We just want what's best for you. I know Clint's absence isn't easy. I felt like I lost a son when we got the news."

The knot in my throat was back. I really wanted him to stop talking. If he continued down that road, I was going break into a million pieces.

"We thought moving you here would be a good thing. No one knows about what happened, and maybe a new set of faces would remind you that life is worth living. I'm starting to think we were wrong. Just give us a chance. You're our only girl. We can't afford to lose you."

"Dad, I'm not going anywhere."

"Then start taking care of yourself, kid."

I nodded but didn't say anything on that note.

"Get on inside," he motioned for the door.

I did as I was told and made my way back to my room. Once in bed, I dreamt about the wolf. Only, instead of watching him run away into the night, I was running with him. We were a pair separated from society and yet considered part of it all at the same time.

It was wonderful.

8

Drake

I WAS SUPPOSED TO BE HUNTING, BUT I COULDN'T STAY AWAY.

On top of that, the call from my contact to see what was going on with the Zealots didn't go as I'd hoped. Apparently Destiny was busy and wouldn't be able to address my issue for several weeks. I could go over her head and ask to speak to Michael, the head archangel. But, no one liked a pissed off Destiny, so I had to bide my time.

But I'd never been known for my patience. I needed Star and the calming effect she had on me. Since she hadn't given me her number, I couldn't call. So, I resorted to sitting at the edge of the clearing behind her house and listened to her sleep. It was becoming sort of a routine.

I felt like a freakin' stalker. But...she'd become mine the moment I met her. If she was hurting, I had to make her feel better. If she was lonely, I had to give her company. Letting her see me in Wolf form had been dangerous, but the cry of her heart beckoned to me. I had to let her know she wasn't alone. If her dad hadn't come out when he had, I'd have walked up to her and let her finally get up close and personal with the Wolf.

I sat in my usual spot just inside the woods and listened to her slow breathing. She was dreaming about the Wolf. It was breathtaking. We ran side by side along a stream in the woods. She was gleaming white. Her green eyes danced with merriment. When we stopped for a break, she nuzzled my neck, and my entire body responded just watching it play out.

Seeing me through her eyes...seeing what could be, made me tilt my head back and howl.

Hell, yeah!

I wanted to strut around and mark every twig and branch within a one hundred mile radius of her house, but instead, I closed my eyes and enjoyed the dream with her.

I'd made my choice. She was mine. Nothing short of death was going to keep me away from her.

Knock it off, Knight. You'll make all the girls go into heat if you keep walking around like that. Mack growled as he approached me. I'd forgotten he was on Star duty tonight.

Ignoring him, I puffed my chest out and continued to strut. *What do you want, Mack?*

Mack sat back on his haunches, a sign of trust. *Word through the ranks is Fate and Destiny are getting involved.*

I'd been the one to contact Destiny, so that part wasn't news to me, but I shook my fur at the mention of Fate. When the fall happened in Heaven, Fate chose the dark side and was appointed second-in-command. She was twisted, sinister, and heartless.

Destiny, Fate's identical twin, on the other hand, usually didn't get involved unless Fate was about to do something catastrophic.

If word was out that the sisters were getting involved, that meant I'd be getting that visit with Destiny sooner than I expected.

What did you hear? I asked him.

Just that. Maybe Fate's working with the Zealots. It wouldn't be the first time she's sided with them.

Who told you the Zealots had been revived?

Meliena.

Of course. She hated Mack, and yet the first chance she got she ran to him. Figured.

Do you think it's something worse? I shifted uncomfortably.

Mack grunted as he shook out his dark brown fur. *It feels like it. Did you get a read on the girl's friends?*

Not really, but if one of them is the leader of the Purists, he or she would know about the mind reading. Mack began to pace. I sat on my haunches and followed his progress.

Crap! I hadn't thought of that. Mack grunted.

I'm thinking we should do a few recon missions to make sure it's not one of them. I grumbled.

Mack halted and cocked his head to the side as he looked at me. *What do you have in mind?*

I was about to tell him I'd meant is as a snide remark, but an idea sparked. *Nothing complicated. Just have some wolves try to pick up their thoughts. I'll send my group inside to see what they can find.*

You know, as sheriff, I should be against Wolf wiretapping. A grin spread across his face. *Do you think the Skunk can handle the pressure?*

I shook my head negatively. *Not Sly. Bugsey and Stella. They're the best in the business for sniffing things out.*

Mack nodded. *Fine. You talk to your group and I'll talk to mine. We'll iron out a plan tomorrow night.*

It's a plan. You going to stay here tonight? He asked. I glanced at Star's house then back at him.

Yeah, I guess.

Mack nodded. *Take care, brother.* And with that, Mack ran off into the night. Once I knew I was alone, I crept up to Star's window she'd left open. The plan had been to shift so I could close the window and quickly shift back without getting caught, but peaking into her brain and seeing she still dreamt of the Wolf sent me into a crazed need to let the world know she was mine.

After I'd marked every tree, bush, and flower around the parameter of her home, I jumped up into her room and curled up next to her on the bed. Not waking from her sleep, she wrapped her arms around me and sighed as she buried her face in my neck.

Right here with Star...this was my heaven.

I closed my eyes, slipping into Star's dream.

Star ran ahead of me as we raced to the water's edge. I wasn't about to tell her I let her win when she turned to give me a proud smile. Right then, I made it my life's mission to keep a permanent smile on her face.

"Do you get to do this all the time?" The awe in her voice was like a vice around my heart. To be able to share this with her was more than I allowed myself to hope for.

"Not all the time," I forced out the words.

"I would. Gah, the freedom! I want to stay like this forever!" She sprinted around me, shaking her white head in the wind.

"It's great, but you have to change back eventually, or the Wolf will take over completely."

"What happens then?"

"You cease to exist. The animal inside controls and eventually your soul dies, leaving the Wolf. But you're still aware. It's weird."

"That's too bad." She frowned, and it was adorable.

"It's fun to be able to live in both worlds." I shrugged before making my way to the running water.

Star moved in beside me, lapping the cold water up with her long, pink tongue. Once we were satisfied, I gave her a small warning before I charged her. She giggled before making a half-hearted attempt of fleeing. I collided into her, sending us to the forest floor in a playful, growling heap. She managed to almost free herself before I finally got my jaw around her jugular. She whimpered in submission, sparking a flame deep inside me.

Unable to stop myself, I let out an answering whine. Freed from my hold, she turned her head and mouthed my muzzle. I bumped my body against hers before turning so I could nibble on her fur. Another whine slipped from her before she positioned her body so she could groom my flank in return.

A quick flick of my tongue in the summer air told me she needed me just as badly as I needed her.

Her body was releasing hormones, giving me the all-clear. The Wolf begged me to make her mine. It desperately needed to take care of his mate in her time of need.

But something held me back. I needed more. I needed her human to tell me she needed me too.

I needed the forever ties of marriage. Only then would I know she was mine for eternity.

She moved so that we were face to face. "Please, Drake," she pleaded.

But it wasn't Star looking at me. It was the Wolf. I wanted her, ached for her, but I couldn't take her like this. She didn't know how real this dream would become. So, instead, I curled up against her.

"Soon," I promised. "Let's enjoy the moment for now."

Her Wolf was reluctant, but I saw the relief in her eyes. We curled up on the ground, letting the sun's rays and the music of our united heartbeats lull us into a peaceful sleep.

❄ 9 ❄

❖

Star

DRAKE HAD GONE MIA. FOR AN ENTIRE WEEK, I FOUND MYSELF scanning the hallways for him even though my brain was telling me to knock it off. I tried focusing on school, but it wasn't the same without him there.

Eight days after the movie, Drake was back. I knew it before I even saw him. He'd filled out. Before, he'd been toned like a soccer player, but now he looked like a Native American version of Thor.

I walked over to where my triangle was without making eye contact with him. That didn't mean I wasn't tempted to look at him. Because the boy sure could fill out a pair of faded blue jeans. And the black t-shirt that looked two sizes too small? Yeah, he definitely had some impressive guns.

A black tattoo danced on his deltoid muscle, catching my eye. Had that always been there?

Despite my resolve not to look at him, I leaned forward to study the intricate body art. At first it just looked like a bunch of swirly lines, but the longer I stared, the more I realized it was some sort of tribal symbol: a wolf head in the center of a moon. Some sort of writing or symbols circled the image. It seemed... otherworldly. Sure, people got some pretty cool tats on those reality ink shows, but this was different. It was almost as if he was born with the mark. I found myself wanting to trace it. To memorize every line and curve of it. If I was honest, part of me, a strong part, wanted to lick him. It was the sexiest thing I'd ever seen.

I'd been having too many wolf dreams lately.

He glanced over at me, causing our eyes to clash and lock. I gasped and immediately averted my attention to my useless triangle.

I didn't play. Mr. Thomas told me it was better to be silent than to try to make up for the cue I always missed. I was content to pull a book out of my bag and read for the next ninety minutes.

"I think you missed your cue." The deep voice almost scared the snot out of me and my book went flying onto the floor. I shot a glare at Drake who towered over me like the Empire State Building.

"I'm not playing," I hissed.

"You will or I'll give you a new lesson. Would you like a repeat of last week?"

"Can't, got grounded." I smiled triumphantly at him. At that moment, I'd never been so happy to be grounded. Any more afternoons like the one we had on the dugout and I'd be a lost cause. His silver eyes were hypnotizing and already I was falling headfirst into his powerful gaze.

"That's fine. I'll just get myself an invite over and we can do the lesson there."

"Grounded means no one can go out and no one can come in." I wasn't sure on the valitiy of my words, but he didn't need to know that. There was no way he was coming over to my house. Just the thought of the two of us alone in my room was doing something to my body that made me squirm in my chair.

"I think if it's for educational purposes, your mom would be more forgiving."

I gave up and bent down to retrieve my book and shoved it into my bag. For the rest of the period I pretended to try, but the entire time I kept wondering what was going on in his head. Why did he care if I could play the dumb triangle? How was I going to protect myself from him in my own home? Would his full lips be as intoxicating as they looked?

What the heck!? Snap out of it, Star!

Once class let out, Drake followed me out to my mother's car.

"Hello, Mrs. Allistar," he smiled charmingly at her. I envisioned that smile was the look a gazelle got right before a cheetah pounced on it.

"Hello, Drake. How are you?"

"Good. I was wondering if it would be okay if I came to the house and gave Star a music lesson. It appears music doesn't come easy for everyone."

"Why, of course you can. We're having meatloaf if you'd like to stay for dinner."

"Well, I think it won't take that long, but thank you for the invitation." He smiled broadly, flashing Mom his perfect white teeth. I watched her face melt and knew she was a lost cause. I was going to have a serious talk with her later.

"Would you like Star to ride with you or me?" Oh, he was good.

"I don't see what riding with you would hurt if you are just coming over to the house. She did tell you she's grounded, right?"

"Yes, only to the house," he nodded.

I grudgingly followed him to his Jeep and slid into the passenger side once he opened the door for me. For the first time, I took note of the condition of the inside of his SUV. It was spotless. The seats were black leather and the tint on the windows was extremely dark. Probably darker than it was legal to be. He had it fully decked out with a built-in GPS, Bluetooth capabilities, and satellite radio. I was impressed.

When he started the car, more Native American music filled the air.

"Which song is this?" I asked, enjoying the mournful feel. It suited me.

"It's the Wolf's. Not the perkiest of the bunch."

"Could you tell me more of the story?"

"Well, there is not much more to tell. When the girl came into the picture, the Wolf found a reason to unite with someone. He sucked at love. Never really knew how to act around her. Pushed her away with his possessiveness."

"Did the Wolf and Bear get along?"

Drake let out a bark of laughter. "No. They almost killed each other in the end."

"Why would they do that? Wouldn't they have some kind of loyalty system since they were both shifters?"

"Are all humans loyal to each other just because they're humans?"

His sarcasm put me in my place. I guess I just assumed they would all bond together for a common good or something like that. Judging by the dark look on his face, I was *waaaay* off.

"Their fighting had nothing to do with the girl's decision to choose neither." He said when I didn't respond.

"Why's that?"

"There was a third part of the equation, a Falcon. I think he was the one who influenced her to choose mortality over the life the bear and wolf could give her."

"Stupid girl," I muttered. "So, were the shifters immortal or something?"

"Something like that. But it doesn't make sense why the Falcon would convince her to stay mortal."

"Why?"

"The Falcon also has the ability to offer...an extended life."

"You know this from experience?"

"No," he chuckled and turned down my street.

"I want to know more about this story, like what the songs are saying."

"There are books on this stuff. You can find it online or at the Reserve bookstore."

I nodded and made a mental note to look it up once he left. The wolf intrigued me. I wanted to know why he chose to stay alone. The whole "extended life" thing had to be bull crap. I didn't believe any of it was real, but I was curious about where the legend came from.

Not to mention that every night since we went to the movies, I dreamt of the wolf I'd seen in the woods. Each dream became more vivid than the last. When I woke up, I could swear I still smelled the Wolf on me.

Weird, I know. But in the dream, all my senses were sharper. I could identify something with my nose and ears miles before I actually saw it. I loved the Wolf's scent. It reminded me of Drake.

Everything about the Wolf reminded me of Drake.

10

༺❀༻

Drake

I PULLED INTO HER PARENTS' DRIVEWAY AND SAW HER DAD standing on the front porch, waiting. The silver hair and deep smile lines were deceiving. There was nothing old about her old man. The dude was huge. If I didn't have superhuman strength, he'd be intimidating as hell. I gave him a slight nod as I put the Jeep in park and prayed he wouldn't give me the third degree. Star and I might not be on a date, but I could still tell I had to pass her father's test of approval. I made damned sure I opened her door for her and let her go up the stairs without taking the opportunity to get a look at her backside. I was going to show him that I'd been practicing manners long before he'd been born.

"Hello, Drake," he nodded once we both stepped onto the porch.

"Good afternoon, Mr. Allistar." I gave him my best smile and extended my hand out to him.

He was quick to shake my hand, squeezing it as hard as he

could before motioning us into the house. I bit the inside of my cheek to keep from smiling. If I'd wanted to, I could turn every bone in his hand into dust. But, that would lose major points with Star.

Kid better watch himself or I'll introduce him to Smith and Wesson.

I had to bite back a chuckle at hearing his thoughts. If only he knew how useless his gun was.

"I see you're off the crutches." Mr. Allistar grunted. I'd forgotten he'd seen me with them the first time I was here. Now I had to get myself out of this mess before he became suspicious.

"Yeah, Doc said my legs are back to normal. No need for the sticks anymore." Okay, so it wasn't original, but judging by the look of acceptance on his face, I knew he bought it. At least one Allistar was easy to convince.

My first thought as we walked into her house was that I needed to stay as far away from her bedroom as possible. I knew I wouldn't play nice if we were behind closed doors. So, I decided the living room was our safest option. We both sat down on the couch and I pulled out the sheet music I'd slipped into my back pocket before we left the band room. It was pathetic that I was using band as a way to get a girl, but it was better than asking her out to dinner or something. That wouldn't fly with her at all. Not yet at least.

"Okay. We'll just use our hands today and clap when you're supposed to *ding*," I said as I placed the music between us so we could both see.

He is so wasting his time. God, why does he have to smell so good?

A satisfied growl rumbled in the back of my throat at hearing her thoughts. I almost felt guilty about listening in on her, but the truth was I couldn't tune her out even if I tried. I'd learned during last week's hunting trip that no matter where I went, I was connected to her. Just thinking about the trip made the Wolf itch. As great as it'd been to let the Wolf out for a week, it'd hurt like hell to be away from Star. It'd been a necessary trip, but that didn't mean I liked it. I wasn't sure the next time I'd be able to hunt like that for a while.

Five minutes into the lesson, I realized she was rhythmically challenged. Seriously. Nothing I did worked. I'd go as slow as possible, counting out each beat and she still missed her note. Every. Time.

Maybe Mr. Thomas was wiser than I'd thought.

I'm so stupid! Why is this so hard for me?

She was beating herself up over something that didn't matter in the grand scheme of things. So, I decided it was time for a little comedic relief.

"Hey, what's that over there?" I asked, pointing at nothing behind her. She spun her head around to see what I'd been looking at, giving me full access to her side. I poked her in the ribs and she let out a squeal, falling into a fetal position.

"Ticklish are we?" I smirked before I dove in for the kill.

Beautiful laughter rang throughout the room as she twisted and convulsed under my attacking fingers. My laughter joined in as a full-on war was waged.

"You'll never take me alive!" She cried as she tried to break free, but I held her down with one hand while I assaulted her with the other. We rolled until I had her pinned beneath me, her green eyes sparkling up at me with merriment. As she giggled and gasped for air, her chest brushed up against mine, and suddenly a whole other area of me was getting involved.

My laughter dried up as I studied her mouth. God, I wanted to kiss her so badly. My thumb brushed against her bottom lip on its own accord. Her laughter slowed as her eyes dropped to half-staff. My head gravitated toward hers. The sound of her spastic heart drummed in my ears. I searched her thoughts but desire consumed her, drowning everything out.

On a groan, I stopped thinking and crushed my lips against hers, bracing her head with my hands as a jolt of energy shot through us at the connection. Although her lips stayed motionless for a few seconds, they quickly caught up to speed and kissed me back with equal fervor. Her hands clung to my arms as she gave as good as she got.

God, it'd never been like this with anyone else. My tongue traced along the line of her closed lips until she opened for me, letting me in to taste the sweetness of her mouth. More. I needed so much more.

My hand slid down her thigh as I moved to link her leg around my waist. She arched against me as her tongue began to duel with mine, and I saw stars when our bodies clashed perfectly.

"Ugh, can I get you both something to drink?"

Shit!

I jumped off Star like she was melting iron and threw myself into the recliner next to the couch before making eye contact with her mom.

Shit. Shit. Double Shit!

I cleared my throat. "I'm fine, Mrs. Allistar. Star?" I turned to see the stunned expression on her face as she sat up, her lips wet and swollen from my kiss, her hair a tumbled, tangled mess from my hands. God, I hoped no one saw how she affected me.

"Nothing." Star whispered as she straightened her shirt.

Mrs. Allistar smirked at us. *It's about time she got over that boy. This one's much cuter.*

"Okay, you let me know if you need anything." Mrs. Allistar waved before walking back into the kitchen.

My blood continued to travel south as I tried to take a few calming breaths. We needed a subject change and fast, or I was going to drag her into her room and give her the release her body was begging for. The room reeked with her desire, causing the edges of my vision to blur.

"I think we're done with the music lesson. Reading in band isn't such a bad thing after all." I tried to smile but it felt forced.

"I'm a master in academics but a disaster in music," Star huffed in defeat.

"That's alright. We can't be perfect at everything." I winked before folding the sheet music back up and sliding it into my pocket.

"What do you fail at?" She challenged.

I gave her a lazy smirk. "Are you insinuating you think I'm perfect?"

She rolled her eyes but a smile still spread across her face. "Don't go getting a big head. It just seems like you excel at whatever you do."

"It just so happens that I suck at knitting. I'm all thumbs." I'd never tried knitting but it was a better alternative to the truth. She didn't need to know I failed at relationships.

Star tilted her head back and laughed. "I'm glad to hear that. It would concern me if you knew how to knit."

"I'll have you know there are several major pro-football players who knit. I'm a total failure."

My heart warmed seeing the smile on her face. It was breathtaking. My new mission in life was to make her smile as many times as I could every single day we were together.

"Anything else I should know about?" She giggled.

I was about to make something else up when her mom came back into the room.

"Drake, will you consider staying for dinner?" The woman was in full-on match-making mode because that was the second time she'd asked that question. Lucky for her, I was in no hurry to go home.

"Yeah, that would be great."

"Do you like meatloaf? Did I already tell you that's what we're having?" Her brow creased in concern.

No reason to point out the obvious, that she'd already mentioned that before. Maybe she had a memory retention issue.

Since cooked meat made me violently sick, I answered, "I'm a vegetarian."

"That's fine. I can whip up a salad for you."

Judging by the "eager to please" look on her face, I knew if I'd said I only liked my meat if it was freshly slaughtered, she would've gone out and wrangled a cow for me. Should've told her the truth. That would've been fun to watch.

"You really don't have to go out of your way for me." I glanced over at Star to see her cute face wrinkled into a frown. What had I done now? I raised an eyebrow at her in silent question. She turned her head away and stared at the blank TV. Her thoughts silent.

"No, I insist. You're willing to give your time up to help Star with her music. It's the least I can do."

Before I could say anything else, Mrs. Allistar was out of the living room and bustling around in the kitchen whistling "Pop Goes the Weasel" using only one pitch.

Now I know where Star gets her musical abilities.

"Okay, so if you aren't into the triangle, what do you like to do?" I asked Star.

"Nothing. I don't like to do anything."

I felt my eyebrows shoot up. "Seriously? What about sports?"

"Nope, nothing."

I sighed and moved so that I was sitting on the couch again. I didn't like the distance between us. "You have to want to do something."

"And why is that?"

I knew I had to be careful with what I said. One wrong word and I'd have an extremely pissed off woman on my hands.

"Well, if you're considering going to college in the fall, you need a fine arts credit, or some sort of extracurricular that would get colleges to notice you."

Her eyes began to tear up, and I panicked.

Shit, what did I say? Why can't I hear her thoughts?

Her face crumbled and giant sobs wracked her tiny frame, making me feel like a freakin' heel. I scooped her up into my arms and cradled her against my chest. Her body shook violently as her hot tears soaked through my shirt. Everything in me screamed to fix the problem, but I had no idea what needed fixing. Suddenly, she bolted from my lap and ran out the back door.

I went after her and found her curled up on the porch swing with her face buried in her hands. The sound of her sobs almost brought me to my knees. I pulled her back into my arms as I sat down on the swing and just rocked us as she let it all out. Finally, I could hear her thoughts again, but they were a jumbled mess. All I could pick up was that she thought she was a failure.

I'd screwed up big time.

"Star, baby, don't cry. I'm sorry." I spoke into her hair as I willed her tears to go away.

"Id naw err aul." Her muffled words vibrated against my chest.

"Yeah, it is my fault. I shouldn't have pushed you so hard. You're smart. That alone is going to catch the eye of whatever college you want to go to."

The harder she cried, the more I realized this was about more than failing at the triangle or not have an extracurricular activity to put on her transcript. It was as if all of her emotions had come to a head and were now exploding all over the place. I rubbed circles on her back, waiting for her to calm down.

"What did I say, Star?" I needed her to talk to me. I needed her to let me in.

"Nothing," she sighed as she looked up at me through pitiful eyes. Her nose was running and her eyes were puffy, and I'd never seen a more beautiful person in all the years I'd been alive.

"You're lying." I know it came out a little harsh, but I needed to get to her somehow.

"Really, it's not your fault. I've just been going through some stuff, and I guess I just snapped." She moved to wipe away her tears, but I beat her to the punch, drying the wet trails with the pads of my thumbs.

"Is this about Clint?" Damn, the second the question was out of my mouth I wished like hell I could take it back. I was in deep, deep crap now.

Her body stiffened, and I held my breath for the explosion.

11

Star

"WHAT?" MY HEAD SNAPPED AND ANGER REPLACED THE SADNESS. "What did my mother tell you?"

"Nothing. It was just a guess," he mumbled as he shifted uncomfortably. Yeah, he'd better be uncomfortable!

"No, don't try to backtrack now. How'd you know about Clint?"

"Dinner is ready," Dad popped his head out the back door.

"Better not keep them waiting." Drake jumped up like he'd just realized he was sitting on hot coals, dumping me on the swing.

I was furious but knew it was not the time to force it out of him. Nothing else made sense other than that my parents told him. Why couldn't they just mind their own business? It was my life...my story to tell.

Dinner was tense. Drake barely ate the salad Mom prepared. I shoved the meatloaf around, but none of it ever made it into my mouth. My parents being oblivious to the tension in the room tried to carry on a conversation.

"So, Drake, what do your parents do?" Dad asked.

Drake swallowed his bite of food before answering, "I was raised by my sister. She's several years older than me and works at the community college."

"Really? What does she do there?" Mom asked, thankfully not addressing the fact he didn't have parents. If Mom decided to make him her project, there'd be no hope for him ever living a peaceful life again. Did that mean he was an orphan? The "outsider" image completely made sense if he was.

Drake gave a slight shrug. "I'm not really sure. A little bit of everything."

"Do you have any plans for college?" Dad asked. It was his standard question for people ages eighteen and under. To him, there was no such thing as being successful without a college degree.

"Um, I'm going to UT in the fall and studying architecture or business administration. I haven't decided yet."

"Good fields. What are your extra-curriculars?"

I glanced up at Drake to see him staring at me. Giving him my best glare, I averted my eyes and went back to spearing my meatloaf.

"I play in the band. I'm not really into school clubs or sports."

"What instrument do you play?" Mom asked.

"Percussion."

He took a deep drink of water, and I hoped he was squirming in his chair. If my parents weren't sitting at the table with us, I'd ream him up one side and down the other until there was nothing left of him but a mass of human flesh. If he wanted to know something about me, he should've come to me instead of poaching my parents for information.

Finally, we finished dinner, and Mom began clearing away the dishes.

"Dinner was very good, Mrs. Allistar." Drake flashed her one of his heart-melting smiles, and my insides boiled at just how tightly he had her wrapped around his finger. Suck up. She had to be the one to spill the beans. Dad wasn't the gossip in the family.

In fact, he rarely carried conversations with people outside the family.

"Please, call me Victoria, and you are welcome to join us anytime."

"I had better get home before my sister starts worrying," Drake said as he stood up.

I had no plans of following him out. He knew the way.

"Walk him to the door," Mom hissed.

I ignored her and went to my room, the opposite direction of the front door. I hated that I felt bad for the way I treated him, and I especially hated how he already knew my secret. I didn't want anyone here to ever know what'd happened. Now, I'd always wonder if he was spending time with me because he wanted to or because he felt sorry for me.

Thanks, Mom and Dad.

⚜

DRAKE PURPOSELY AVOIDED ME ALL WEEK. I TRIED TO GET HIS attention in band, but he always acted like he didn't see or hear me. In the hallways, he'd pretend he was in deep conversation with whomever he was walking with so he wouldn't notice me. I'd left two notes in his locker giving him my cell number and telling him we needed to talk, but I never heard back from him.

Several times Wayley and Onyx called me out on how I always looked over my shoulder for him. It felt like he was all around me yet never close enough to see. I was going crazy!

When Friday rolled around and I still hadn't gotten Drake alone, I decided to take matters into my own hands.

Mom was unusually late in picking me up. So, I parked myself beside Drake's Jeep until she came. I pulled out my Kindle and started reading the book of Cherokee legends I'd downloaded last night. In the middle of reading about Beaver's Grandchild and his search for dry land at the dawn of creation, a shadow cast over my hands. I looked up to see Drake looming in front of me.

"Are you going to give me answers today?" I asked dryly.

"No." He didn't even blink when he said it. No explanation. No apology. No guilt. Nada!

It took everything in me not to strangle his neck. "Just tell me one thing, was it my mother?"

"No, and not your father either."

"Then how..." If it wasn't my parents who told him, how did he know? I wasn't linked to Clint's story. His parents made sure of that. *None* of the newspapers even mentioned me. I looked up at him, taking in each feature as if it was the first time I'd ever seen him. Who was this guy, and how had he so totally consumed my thoughts in such a short period of time? How did he know so much about me?

"When are your restrictions up?" Seriously? After not talking to me for a week, that's what he asks me?

I wanted to say something snarky and tell him where he could shove his question, but it felt so good to have him speaking to me again. Standing this close to him brought back memories of our tickle fight on the couch. And that kiss? I went liquid just thinking about how potent his lips had been, how possessive his hands had been. I wanted to see where this thing between us was going. Clint was still in my heart, but a shift was happening inside me. I was starting to believe in the ability to love two people.

Not that I was in love with Drake! God, it was too soon for that...right?

"It depends." I shrugged. "If you were Wayley or Onyx, you'd have to wait another two weeks. Because you are you, my punishment sentence probably never even began. My mom worships the ground you walk on."

I eagerly waited for a smile to spread across his face, but nothing happened. Why was he even mad in the first place? I was the one with the right to be upset, not him!

"Have you read up on the bear-wolf legend, yet?"

"Just downloaded the book last night. Right now, I'm reading the creation story."

"Once you finish the book, call me."

This conversation was confusing the heck out of me. Why did he want to know when I would be ungrounded? What did that have to do with reading up on the legend we'd talked about? I felt like I needed a degree in astrophysics to understand him.

"Ooh-kaaay. Then give me your number. Can't call unless I have that." I smirked at his retreating back.

Still nothing.

He stopped, turned around, and came back to me. Grabbing my phone out of my hand, he tapped furiously on the screen for all of five seconds before handing it back to me. Without saying another word, he turned and climbed into his Jeep. I stepped back enough to allow him to pull out of his space. As he drove off, I couldn't help but wonder if things would ever be good between us. It seemed like every time we moved passed one barrier, something else came up to cause more problems.

Once he was out of sight, I looked down at my phone to see that he'd changed my wallpaper. It was black screen with three little words written in white block lettering.

You own me.

Strange, yet oddly exciting. This boy was short-circuiting my brain!

That night, I pulled out my Kindle and skipped over to the chapter on the legend between the Bear, Falcon, and Wolf. I discovered there was much more to the story than Drake let on. According to the author of my book, no one really knew how the girl died. There were some who believed she killed herself. Others claimed she died of the plague. A third category linked her death to a cult that used her as a virgin sacrifice. That one made me snort.

The most intriguing part of the legend was the people who had the ability to shift from human to animal and were called Guardians. The Bear was the chief of the small tribe in Cherokee, North Carolina while the Wolf was the chief of a tribe further north. Both tribes were Cherokees by blood but neither ever worked together. The Falcons in the story were part of a sect that broke away from the Aztec tribe and colonized in Europe. Not much was said about them, which made me wonder about their existence. Maybe that part of the story had been fabricated. My guess was the Falcon was a settler in the area who fell in love with the girl.

The Bear was a large man with unusual strength. He had the ability to control people's emotions. His destiny was to guard the mountains and keep them safe. He eventually married one of the Elder's daughters and their lineage continued. Some sources claimed Bear was the gentle monster, never attacking anyone but still turning into an animal when enraged. He was known for destroying things when he saw his people mistreated. Obviously he failed, because the Native Americans had been forced off their land during the Trail of Tears.

The Wolf apparently never married. When the girl was no longer in the picture, he disappeared. Some claimed to have seen him while others discredit his existence. He was large and dark as the night. He had a keen sense of smell and the ability to read his prey's thoughts. Supposedly, he and his tribe were placed on the earth to protect the people that inhabited it, but something happened to make him stop. Some believed when hikers went missing, it was because he ate them. Others reported the Wolf killed the Falcon the girl loved, leading to her suicidal death. Where the Bear had been surrounded by friends and family, the Wolf was completely alone.

I read and re-read the legend but was unsatisfied. Why did all this matter to Drake? It was just some silly campfire entertainment.

Picking up my cell, I dialed his number. A female's voice answered on the other end.

"Is Drake there?" my voice croaked.

Lord, please don't let her be his girlfriend. I couldn't handle that right now.

"No...he's out right now. May I ask who's calling?" She sounded unsure of herself. Was that a sign? Was he already taken? An unexpected surge of jealousy laced with possessiveness almost knocked the air out of me. I'd never experienced anything like it, not even when girls would flirt with Clint in front of me.

"Um, could you just tell him Star called and to have him call me back?"

"Sure." I heard the phone click and tossed my phone onto the bed.

Well, that was interesting.

I tried doing homework, but my mind kept going back to the mysteries of the legend. Was Drake trying to say he was a descendant of the Bear? He didn't fit the description of the Bear. He couldn't be the Wolf. He was too big for that. Was he the Falcon?

I heard wheezing and realized it was coming from me. The room suddenly began to spin as I gasped for air that never came. I forced my head between my legs and tried to calm myself down. I was freaking out over a stupid legend that wasn't real. Storytelling is what they did back then. What else were they going to do? They didn't have cable or Facebook or Netflix.

Even as I struggled to take in deep breaths, I had to snort at my randomness. Yes, because Facebook and Netflix were the places where all social activity happened. (That was sarcasm, fyi.)

Once I'd gotten myself under control, I decided I needed to go to bed before my mind could come up with any other scenarios. Unfortunately, as soon as I stretched out onto my bed, I was wide awake. After an hour of tossing and turning, my phone rang.

"You called?" the deep voice on the other line asked once I made a groggy sound that was supposed to be a greeting.

"Huh?"

"My sister said you called. Did you?"

"Drake? What time is it?" I rolled over and saw that it was only eleven.

"Did you read up on the legends?"

"Yeah, sounded like a bunch of myths to me."

He was silent for a moment then asked, "Can you go with me somewhere tomorrow?"

"I don't know. Why don't you just come over and ask my parents?"

"Okay. Tomorrow."

Before I could ask him any of the questions running through my head, he hung up. I wanted to hunt him down and demand some answers but decided it would be better for everyone involved if I got some sleep first.

I dreamt I was the girl from the legend and three men were fighting for my attention, Drake being one of them. None of them ever changed forms, but I knew they were capable of it. I screamed, begging them to stop, but they ignored me as they ripped each other apart limb by limb. I woke up with a gasp when the fighting stopped and they turned, preparing to pounce on me.

❧ 12 ❧

Star

AT 7:30 A.M., THERE WAS A KNOCK AT THE FRONT DOOR. I groaned, already knowing who it was. The front door opened and a deep voice mumbled something. Mom's high pitched voice answered in delight.

Drake was here.

I buried myself under the covers, praying for an extra few minutes of sleep. But, Mom stormed into my room with a burst of energy. Giggling like a freakin' school girl.

"Rise and shine, sweetie. You have a visitor."

Knowing my protests would be pointless, I rolled out of bed and grabbed a pair of black skinny jeans, my black *Guns and Roses* t-shirt, and my favorite black hoodie jacket on the way to the bathroom. One look in the mirror and I squeaked. My hair was a mess! I quickly ran a comb through it, but all the curl had teased out to the point of no return, making it look like I had one impressive fro. As I tried to come up with a solution for my hair, I brushed my teeth. I finally gave up and decided to pull it all back into a messy bun. Even then, I was pretty sure cavewomen had better hair than me.

When I walked out into the living room dressed and as ready as I was ever going to be, I spotted Drake sitting in my dad's recliner wearing faded jeans and a green hoodie. His hair was out of its usual ponytail and hung in a damp shaggy mess around his face an inch above his shoulders. I could smell his soap from where I stood, and I wanted to get closer for a better sniff. Lord, I needed to stop dreaming about Wolves. I was starting to think like one! But the man definitely reeked with sexiness.

At the risk of sounding cliché, Drake looked larger than life in my parents' little living room. I felt a contradictory energetic jolt in my stomach that was way too perky for morning as I took in every impressive inch of him. Yeah, so maybe he was right. Girls did think with their...ahum, you know...every now and then. Because I definitely was at the moment.

"Ready?" he gave me a knowing grin as he stood up. Was I that transparent? Or had I said something out loud? Oh God, what if I had?

"Sure," I shrugged with a calmness I definitely didn't feel.

"Don't worry about curfew," Mom waved as we walked out the door.

In the passenger seat of the Jeep was a brown bag. At my raised brow, Drake commanded, "Open it."

Not needing to be told twice, I unfolded the top to find a warm, gooey cinnamon bun practically smiling up at me. My mouth watered instantly.

"Thanks." My voice sounded skittish and awkward, as if I'd never spoken to him before. Maybe his consideration made me a little giddy inside. Okay, I was doing freakin' toe-touches in my mind. Cinnamon buns were my kryptonite!

"I wasn't sure what you'd like. My sister kept trying to get me to bring a scone, but I wasn't sure what it was, so I went with the one that had the most sugar."

"You chose well." Good, that sounded more like me. I wanted to give him a hug and tell he'd hit buttery, sugary, cinnamon gold... but that would be awkward. Especially since we hadn't spoken much to each other since our kiss a week ago.

I pulled off a piece of the bun and allowed the buttery, cinnamon concoction to melt on my tongue. It was heaven. I had to fight hard to hold back the moan of pleasure wanting to spill out. Again, groaning in front of a boy I was interested in would be a tad bit...what's the word I'm looking for? Awkward! Not to mention borderline porno.

A sudden mental image that involved him and me and the cinnamon bun with cheesy saxophone music in the background while he did kinky things involving said pastry made me blush to my roots. Lord, where had my mind gone?!

Keep it PG, Star!

"Where are we going?" I asked after I'd licked every drop of icing off my fingers.

"You'll just have to wait and find out."

We rode in silence while I finished the best cinnamon bun I'd ever eaten. Once that was all gone, I became extremely bored with the silence.

"Do you mind if I turn on the radio?" I asked.

"Sure." We both reached for the radio and our hands bumped. I let out a nervous laugh as a bolt of electricity shot through me.

Get it together! I scolded myself.

"You go ahead. It's your car."

He turned it on to a station that played a variety of music, and I snuggled back into the chair and took in a whiff of fresh leather.

"The bruises are gone. Is your nose still sore?" he asked.

"What? Oh, I completely forgot about it. I think it only hurts if I push on it. Other than that, no pain."

"Good."

"I think you have the hardest chest of anyone I know." After the words left my mouth I wished I hadn't said them. I meant it as a mere observation, but it came out sounding like a lame pick-up line. Although, I definitely hadn't minded the view I got when he gave me his shirt. *Mmmm!*

"You must have hit a bone."

"You know, this Jeep doesn't fit you. You seem more like the fast car or motorcycle type of guy," I said, changing the subject.

"You're more accurate than you think," he winked but didn't say anything else.

Drake suddenly turned off the road and my head slammed into the roof of the Jeep. I screamed as my hand clamored for the "oh crap" bar. The world blurred before me as the SUV shook violently. We were going to die! I just knew it. If this was a road, it needed some serious TLC, but it felt like we were plunging down a ravine to our untimely deaths. Drake's massive arm whipped out in front of me, pressing my body back into the seat just before he skidded to an abrupt stop. Had he not done that, I was certain my head would've gone through the windshield.

"Home." How the heck did he sound so calm when we almost turned into tree ornaments? They needed to get that problem fixed ASAP.

Drake hopped out and hurried over to my side of the Jeep and opened the door. The first step was the hardest. My knees were shaking so bad they buckled under my weight, forcing me to cling to his hand. Once I had my bearings again, I took in my surroundings. A quaint log cabin that looked to be made out of Lincoln logs sat nestled in the woods. Lace blinds decorated the windows and a red berry wreath hung on the green door.

As we stepped onto the front porch, I looked down at the doormat that read, "Welcome." Empty pots lined the porch steps, just waiting to be filled after the last frost. Two rocking chairs sat lonely on either side of the entryway.

Drake twisted the knob, pushing the door open with his foot as he motioned for me to go in. Inside smelled like baked bread and cinnamon. A slender woman with a long braid draped down her back emerged from the kitchen with a broad smile on her face.

"You must be Star. I'm Meliena, this lug's sister."

I shook her extended hand.

"Nice to meet you," I smiled sheepishly. I felt like a hulk next to her slender frame. I mean, seriously, she reminded me of a Native American fairy from Pixie Hollow.

"Come in. I just made some bread and spiced tea. Would you like some?"

I was stuffed and slightly nauseous but didn't know how to decline gracefully. Drake stepped in for me. "She had one of your cinnamon buns on the way over. Maybe later."

"Yes. It was amazing." I smiled shyly.

"That's fine. Make yourself at home, Star."

Meliena had a hypnotic presence about her. I couldn't help but feel suddenly at ease around her. I should've felt a little nervous meeting his family, especially considering her hostile treatment when I called last night. Instead, I was experiencing the peace that comes from relaxing in an amazing hot tub.

Weird.

Drake as he led me to a room that looked like a cross between a library and a living room. Books were shelved from the floor to the ceiling along every wall with the exception of the space cut out for the window, but a massive sectional, a large leather chair, and side tables dominated the center of the room.

There were no family pictures anywhere. Evidence to his loneliness. He understood what it meant to lose your world. Maybe it was the reason for why we were drawn to each other. I wanted to ask him what happened to his parents but felt like I would be overstepping my boundaries. Besides, I didn't want to talk about Clint just yet, and Drake was the type to expect reciprocation when talking about the hard stuff. Not that I'd ever gotten him to talk like that, but I knew he'd demand it if we ever did. It was just a feeling I had inside me.

He sat down on the couch, motioning for me to do the same.

"How much older is your sister than you?" I remained standing. I knew the second I sat next to him all rational thoughts would flee my brain. Ask questions first. Stare mindlessly at sexy boy second.

"Not much." His eyes shifted away from me and he stared vacantly out the window. I recognized that move. I used it on my parents all the time when I wanted to avoid the issue.

He was hiding something. If his parents' deaths really happened a long time ago and she wasn't that much older than him...that meant they were orphans living alone in this house when they were just kids. Suddenly, the place didn't look so quaint. The delicate quilts hanging through heart-shaped wooden rings mocked me with a past that didn't exist. The painted signs about home and hearth were all a lie. This wasn't a place of welcome. This was a refuge for the broken and abandoned.

"So, you said you thought the legend was a myth. What makes you think that?" he asked once I finally sat down on a leather chair across from him. My knees had given out on me at some point during my freakout.

When the silence finally hit me, I realized it was the first time I'd been completely alone with a guy since Clint. The dugout incident didn't count because we were still on school property. And the times in his Jeep didn't count because his attention was always divided between me and the road.

Drake looked far too good at the moment as he stretched out on the couch, his jeans hugging him just right, giving me a good idea of what his impressive thigh muscles looked like. I could feel my resistance barrier crumbling more and more as the seconds dragged on.

What was his question again?

Oh, right. The stupid legend.

"Well, the author seemed so speculative. He bounced around with different opinions but never really gave anything concrete. If it was all true, wouldn't there be a definite answer?"

"Do you always need hard evidence to understand truth? Didn't you believe in Santa as a kid?"

"Nope. My parents didn't believe in the disillusionment of childhood. I got presents at Christmas, but it was always from Mom and Dad. Not Santa, Mrs. Claus, or the elves. Why do you care? You seemed to agree with me earlier that it was just a crazy story."

"Okay, Santa wasn't a good example." Drake sighed and raked his fingers through his shaggy hair. "Do you believe in God?"

I frowned at him as I tried to follow his train of thought. The boy had the ability to twist my brain into knots with a few simple words. "I'm not entirely sure. I mean, I believe in the existence of a higher being but *God*...I don't know."

"Never mind. This whole thing is stupid." He jumped to his feet and shoved his hands into his pockets as he began to pace. A dark hank of hair fell into his face, making him look like James Dean, only sexier.

"Look, I don't believe humans can change into animals and back again. It's not scientifically possible. I don't believe in people who feed off human blood by night and sleep in coffins by day. Those are just stories created to scare little kids witless."

"What if it was all true? What if you found out you were seriously wrong? Not the blood drinkers who sleep in coffins thing, but the shifters."

"What if the sky turned lime green? What if we grew extra feet? What if the cafeteria served real food? It's just a game of 'what if.' I'm sorry if I'm offending you. You can believe this stuff if you want. I don't. I respect you, but I don't have to believe with you."

He was pacing back and forth in front of the window. I gave up trying to read his expression because the dim glow from the cloudy sky formed a silhouette around him, darkening his face. A growl came from him, and I wondered if he was super pissed or just hungry. I was going with the first option at the moment. My fists clenched at my sides, and I prepared myself for what was to come.

"Star, one day you're going to realize the world doesn't revolve around you; that there is an entire universe out there that doesn't make sense but exists nonetheless. I just hope you're ready for it when it happens."

"What the heck does that mean? What makes you think-"

"Drake, we've got company," Meliena said as she ran into the room.

"Yeah, I know," he muttered and stalked away.

"What'd he mean by that?" I turned to Meliena, still shaken by his anger. I knew I was missing something, but I just couldn't figure it out. Looking into her warm brown eyes, I felt instant peace.

Odd.

"You really don't know? Why would he bring you *here* of all places if he didn't tell you?" Meliena frowned.

"I don't know! No one is telling me anything. It's really starting to tick me off! He just went on about that stupid legend. Who cares?!" I fought against the serenity with everything in me.

"I think if you just let all the information process, you'd find your answer. Right now, we need to get you into the basement."

"What?" I squeaked and jumped to my feet. Now I was getting nervous and extremely anxious, like I was expecting someone to come at me wearing a hockey mask and wielding a chainsaw.

"Our visitors aren't friendly. You'll be safer down there."

I followed without resistance. After this was all over, I was going to demand Drake tell me everything. If I had to hide in his damp basement, he owed me that much. As we passed a window, I glanced out to see what looked like a pack of massive wolves surrounding a black one crouched down with its hackles raised.

"Ohmigod," I gasped.

Meliena shoved me through a door. I tripped over the first step, but caught myself on the second one.

"If you want to live. Don't. Make. A. Sound." Meliena warned before slamming the door.

I slid down to the bottom of the stairs and pulled myself up into a ball, rocking back and forth to keep from whimpering.

❧ 13 ❧

❧

Drake

I SCREWED UP BIG TIME BY BRINGING STAR TO MY HOUSE AND Mack was pissed.

I shifted in midair, landing on my haunches in front of him. My lips curled back into a snarl as a warning growl rumbled deep in my chest. The pack circled me, gnashing their teeth. I kept my eyes trained on their alpha. My subordinate. His gold eyes sparkled with rage as foam dripped through his exposed canines.

When were you planning on telling me the Falcons were back?

I fought back the urge to smirk at his use of the Alpha voice on me. The pup seriously thought he could usurp the Supreme? I rose to my full height, staring him down.

"If your guys were on the East end last night like they were supposed to be, you would've known. It's not like you to slack off."

Last night had sucked royally. Meliena sent out the alert that two teenagers had disappeared off the Ramsey Cascades trail. I'd spent two hours scaling the entire mountain until I finally found one of their backpacks ripped to shreds and covered in blood. A quick sniff told me the owner of the bag hadn't made it.

Whoever had done it wanted it to look like an animal had torn the person limb by limb, but no animal touched that bag.

I'd followed the scent from the bag to a deep ravine and found two dismembered bodies lying beside each other, their dead, lifeless hands linked together. Like they'd clung to each other in the face of death, prepared to cross over together. I recognized the boy as one of the teens from the Reservation. The girl had black hair and pale skin, but I hadn't allowed myself to get any closer to take in the rest of her features.

Someone had left them for me to find. The resemblance between the two teenagers and Star and me didn't go unnoticed. It was a warning.

What little food I had in my system had made a second appearance before I sent a message out to Meliena to let her know where to lead the search party. I wanted to find the bastard that killed two defenseless teenagers and make him pay with his own life.

It looked like a scene of a brutal animal attack, but it'd been a long time since an animal larger than a rabbit was in the vicinity of where the unfortunate couple was found.

In the midst of my angry pacing as I'd waited, I caught a strong whiff of leather and cinnamon. The only souls alive with that smell were Falcons.

I climbed to the highest point possible and looked down in the valley below to spot two human-sized Falcons feeding on a deer. Thankfully, the wind had been blowing west, carrying my scent away from them. Otherwise, it would have been a two-against-one fight, and I wouldn't have stood a chance.

By the time Meliena arrived, I was nowhere to be found. Instead, I went home and called Star, desperately needing to hear her voice. I had to hear for myself that she was okay.

Deep down inside was the knowledge that I didn't stand a chance with her. Raeb had the tribe to back him. The Sterlings were stinking rich and could buy the world if they wanted. I was just a screw up.

But that wasn't going to stop me from trying.

Mack snorted, bringing me back to the situation. He shook his head hard as he lowered further, preparing himself for a pounce.

One of them killed Nico this morning. Deal's off, Drake. I can't let the girl kill my pack.

Nico was Mack's cousin. He'd been hotheaded and quick-tempered. He probably thought he could take on much more than he could chew, and it came to bite him in the butt. Still, it sucked he died at Falcon hands.

I'm sorry, Mack. You know you can't blame this on Star. She's an innocent. I snarled when he took a step toward me.

Move out of the way, Drake.

My hackles went on red alert as I prepared to go for his jugular. If he tried to take one step past me, I was going to rip his head off. No one was touching Star. He and I both knew I could control him if he pushed the issue.

Back the hell away, Mack. I gave him one last chance to stand down before I brought the Supreme Alpha forward.

She's going to get us all killed, Drake. You're an idiot if you don't see that.

It's not her fault this is happening! You leave her out of this. If you've got a problem, you deal with me. Got that?

Mack glared at me but made no move in my direction. I stood between him and the entrance to the cabin. If he tried anything, I'd kill him and think about the consequences later. I watched the war rage in his eyes as he stared me down. I let the Supreme flash in my eyes and watched with satisfaction as he jerked his eyes away.

Message received.

If one more of my family dies, deal's off. Mack growled one last time before he ran off, the others falling in line behind him.

Just before he disappeared over the bluff, he turned back to me.

It's your family, too, you know?

I shook my head in frustration. *I lost my family a long time ago. Those are just posers.*

I didn't bother giving an order. He and I both knew he'd given a pack promise. Nothing short of our deaths could break it. Today had just been an act of grief.

I walked into the barn where I kept an extra pair of clothes. By the time I re-entered the house, Meliena was sitting in the living room with a deep scowl on her face.

"I can't believe you brought her here without telling her first. How stupid can you be?" She hissed under her breath.

"Save it, Meliena. I don't need you to tell me what I already know." I held my hand up to silence any further protests as I marched over to the door to the basement.

My heart stopped beating when I opened it and found Star huddled in a fetal position at the bottom of the steps. She was rocking herself, humming a song under her breath. My chest constricted, and it took everything in me not to scoop her up into my arms. Unfortunately, some things needed to be dealt with first. Only then could I claim the right to touch her again.

I silently prayed she didn't run out the house screaming.

14

※

Star

"COME ON, STAR! DON'T BE A CHICKEN!" CLINT SHOUTED FROM THE *water below.*

Easy for him to say. He thought racing motorcycles on little dirt roads was mild entertainment.

I clung to the thick rope in my hands as my body convulsed with nerves.

"You promise the water's deep?"

"Baby, I wouldn't lie to you. Just let er' fly."

His deep Southern drawl washed over me, having the calming effect I needed. With a loud squeal, I ran until the ground disappeared and all I had was the rope chafing my hands. Right before I started to swing back in the direction of the cliff, I let go, plunging down into the freezing cold water.

For a second, I couldn't tell up from down. I opened my mouth to scream, ingesting a deep gulp of nasty lake water as I flailed around. When I was ready to give up and let the water take me down, strong hands grabbed me under the arms and yanked me to the surface.

"Don't scare me like that!" Clint barked as he shoved the hair out of my face to look me over.

I should've been freaked out. I should've been pissed it had taken him so long to help me. Instead, a giggle surged forward until I was laughing so hard I couldn't breathe.

"It's not funny, Star. You could've drowned!" Clint chastised me as he held me tight against him.

"But I didn't, and that was fun," I said once the laughter subsided into random hiccups and giggles.

"Star, I couldn't live with myself if you died," he whispered into my ear so none of his friends could hear.

"But you won't have to, 'cause I'm not going anywhere," I smiled up at him reassuringly.

"Promise me." He demanded, his serious sea green eyes robbing away the last strains of laughter right out of my chest.

I cupped his face with my hands. "I promise."

His lips clamped onto mine as he sealed the deal with a kiss that ended way too soon.

"Get a room!" Gage yelled from his perch on a large bolder to our right.

While Clint was preoccupied sending his friend the death glare, I used it to my advantage, shoving him beneath the water. When he popped up spurting water, there was a sinister gleam in his eyes.

"You're going to get it, babe," he warned just before he lunged.

☙❧

"THEY'RE GONE." DRAKE'S DEEP VOICE BROKE INTO THE memory.

I tried to move, but I couldn't. My legs felt like they were made of Jell-O. He came down the steps and effortlessly hoisted me up into the air, carrying me up the steps. Just being able to breathe in his pine, citrus scent was calming my frazzled nerves.

I was safe.

Unfortunately, he released me as soon as he reached the living room and took a step back to put some space between us. I gave my head a shake to clear away the cobwebs before asking, "How did you get rid of those wolves? You were completely outnumbered."

He didn't answer.

As I scanned my eyes over him, inspecting every inch to reassure myself he hadn't been eaten or mauled by wolves, I realized he'd changed into a dark pair of jeans and a black t-shirt that stretched precariously over his chiseled, unmarred chest. Good to know he worried about a wardrobe change while I was holed up in his basement. But I had to admit, he looked good in that shirt.

Something stirred in me when I was around Drake. Something I thought had died with Clint: desire. It felt good, and for the moment, I allowed it to be there.

I was staring, and he knew it. When my eyes made contact with his heated gaze, I jerked my focus to the window, more specifically to a clump of clothes lying in the grass. It took some squinting, but I finally made out what it was: a shredded green hoodie and tattered faded jeans.

"Did you...did you fight those wolves? How come you aren't hurt? Don't you know they're dangerous? Are there even wolves in this part of the country?" I started rambling hysterically. The thought of Drake, a mere human who'd only weeks ago needed crutches to get around only weeks ago, trying to fight off a hungry pack of wolves had closed off all my airways.

His sinister chuckle broke through my internal meltdown.

"Of course I know their potential, and technically, no, there aren't any wolves in the area."

"Then why'd you go out there? And how are they here?"

"They're looking for me." He only answered my first question.

"What? None of this is making any sense! How would you know what a wolf wah..." Then it all came down on me, the force of it doubling me over at the waist. He was hard as a rock, lean, swift, masculine. He was always alone with the exception of his sister. He knew things about me I'd never told him...as if he'd read my mind. An image of the huge wolf in my yard flashed before me. It was him!

"It was you I saw that night!" I gasped and was suddenly terrified of the one person who made me feel safe. I vaguely remembered reading that werewolves killed humans. Thankfully, it wasn't a full moon, but still, I was paralyzed with fear.

"We don't need a full moon to change." I could hear the smirk in his voice.

"Oh my god, oh my god, oh my god," I began whimpering. "Please don't eat me." I straightened and backed myself up against a bookshelf. He positioned himself between me and any means of escape, caging me in with his arms.

So this is what a rabbit felt in the face of a hungry Wolf. Good to know.

He tilted his head back and a bark of laughter escaped him. "You are the last person I would ever eat; if I ate people...which I don't."

"What about all those missing hikers from the legend? If it's all true."

"They weren't missing because of me. I tried to find them. Usually, I'm too late." Sadness etched deep into his features.

"Wh-what do you mean? Is there something else out there worse than you?"

He laughed, but it looked like he was in pain. As if my words were tearing him apart.

"I'm not a monster, Star."

His broken words made me wince. I was handling this all wrong, but it wasn't every day a girl finds out the boy she's crushing on is a man-wolf.

Patience flashed in his silver eyes as he watched me fall to pieces. "How are you acting so calm?" I sputtered.

"I've had several years to adjust to the news." He grinned sardonically.

I laughed dryly.

"You're still not getting it, are you?" He pressed himself against me. All the blood in my brain went elsewhere as soon as our bodies made contact, robbing me of my ability to think.

"Get what? That you are a freakin' man-wolf-boy?"

He lowered his face so that his lips were just a breath away from mine. "You're the girl, Star."

"Wh-what?" I squeaked. "I can't be the girl. That myth, if true, happed almost a thousand years ago. Oh my god, you're over a thousand years old!" It was all too much. The room was spinning, I really wanted to kiss him, and I heard his ironic laughter. This went down in the books as the strangest thing to ever happen to me. And this from a girl who grew up in Atlanta.

"No, it only happened about three hundred years ago." He stroked my cheek.

"Oh, much better," I answered dryly.

"And it was your great-great-great-great aunt who was the original girl. No reincarnation here."

"You're wrong. My ancestors came from England one hundred years ago. It can't be me. You're wrong." I knew I was rambling and repeating myself, but I just couldn't get myself to accept what he was telling me. I mean, who could?

I felt a gentle hand on my shoulder and turned to look into Meliena's understanding brown eyes. I jerked away from her as if she was a hot stove, which caused me to crash into Drake's arm. He pulled me flush up against him, keeping me steady.

Okay, I was reacting to all this like a total wimpy girl. For some reason, it was my autopilot response.

"That's what Helena's parents wanted everyone to believe. They were humiliated by what happened," Meliena explained.

"What ha-happened?" I knew I needed to hear the story and finally get it through my thick skull.

"Helena supposedly fell in love with one of us, but we never knew who. I found her dead in a ravine. Her wagon flipped over somehow. Raphael, the Falcon, couldn't live with himself. He came to me and begged me to kill him. Claimed if he couldn't spend eternity on earth with Helena, he'd spend eternity in Heaven with her. I didn't want to do it, but once a shifter decides to die and makes the request, there is nothing anyone else can do to change it if it's approved by the Creator." Drake sighed deeply as he ran his fingers through his hair.

"Her family didn't want anyone to know their daughter was involved with such nonsense, so they went back to England and stayed there for a generation. They made sure no one ever knew what happened," Meliena finished.

"So, you, this person holding me, can turn into a Wolf, and there really was a Falcon, and there is some person out there who can transform into a bear?"

"That would be Sam's descendants, yes. And there *are* Falcons. Present tense and plural. Just because Raphael is gone doesn't mean they're all gone. He had a twin brother, Brighton, who tries to hunt me down from time to time. The Wolves who came today are also shifters and were warning me that he's back."

"So, why was I shoved into a basement if that's all they had to say?"

Drake grimaced as he began to pace. "They think killing you will save the pack. One of their brothers died at Sterling hands this morning. If too many Falcons come into the area, there could be a war."

War? Why did there have to be a war? Why couldn't I just finish out my days like a normal high school teenager? It was moments like this I missed Clint. He had his problems, but at least he didn't turn into a freakin' animal!

"I need to go home. This is all too much," I sighed as I rested my head on his shoulder. Yes, in the midst of my world crumbling, I still felt anchored in his arms.

That was messed up.

"Do you think you can stand on your own?" he asked, hesitating to remove his arms from me.

"I'm fine," I snapped as I forced myself out of his grasp.

When I looked into his blue eyes, I realized I'd hurt him emotionally with my behavior. He had to live with the fact he was a monster every day. I wasn't helping any. Deep regret saturated his beautiful face. I wanted so badly to reach up and touch his cheek in reassurance. But...I wasn't sure if I could trust my instincts right now. He may still be the same person I knew an hour ago, but now that I knew the truth, everything changed for us.

"I'm not a monster, Star." I almost hadn't heard it, but before I could respond, he spun on his heels and marched out the door.

I followed him out to the Jeep and let myself in rather than waiting for him to help me. Once he was in on his side, I turned to look at him.

"Why did you feel the need to tell me about this? I was just fine living in oblivion."

"To protect you." At first, I thought he was going to leave it at that. He cranked the vehicle to life and put it in drive. Once we were clear of the driveway from hell and back onto the main road, he continued. "History is going to repeat itself. Your family has been gone from this area for generations, but now you're back. Helena made mistakes that killed her. I can't let that happen to you."

"Choose the Falcon over you? Um, I don't think I'll be that stupid."

"You don't understand. We're made to attract you. It's a luring tactic designed by Fate."

"Who is Fate?"

"The leader of *Shadowmen*, the coven of evil shifters. She set the whole thing up, but when we didn't die, I'd assumed the curse was broken. Apparently not."

"Um, okay. So you're saying I will like all of you? Well, news-flash, I don't like anyone." That wasn't exactly true, but now was not the time for a heart-to-heart revelation.

"Because of Clint."

Hearing his name on someone else's lips was strange but didn't induce the reaction I'd expected. Apparently my current situation was taking dominance over the grief. I was riding in a SUV with a werewolf who could eat me if he wanted, despite his earlier reas-surances to the contrary.

"I'm not a werewolf, Star. I'm a shifter. There's a huge difference."

"You read my mind, didn't you?"

"It's unintentional where you're concerned," he muttered.

"You're going to have to explain yourself, considering the fact I'm new to your world and all." I glowered at him.

"The second you walked into the band room, our brains clicked. I haven't been able to get you out of my head since then."

"Then you understand why history can't repeat itself. Clint was my life. When he died, he took my heart with him. I'm not sure I can handle that kind of heartbreak again."

"You'd be surprised what time can do."

"I can't believe you'd say that! It's so cliché, and besides, I honor my word. I can't just forget about him. That would be wrong."

"I don't know how to say this to you without sounding cold. Clint is gone. He's not coming back. Are you going to spend the rest of your life honoring a memory, or are you going to show him you can live without him?"

I was careful not to let my thoughts go to all the times today I'd checked Drake out. Or how often I'd thought about our kiss. He didn't need to know just how affected I already was by him. He was right. Clint wasn't coming back, and the reality was all my arguments were half-hearted at best. Drake gave me the strength to think about moving on. Yes, I still missed Clint like crazy. He'd been my best friend long before he was my boyfriend. He was the one I turned to when things got rough at home. He'd been my biggest fan.

I watched Drake grip the steering wheel as his jaw clenched. I realized I wasn't doing a very good job of hiding my thoughts. *Sorry about that*, I thought and watched him turn and smirk. It was all too much, but I figured if I tried to go along with it, maybe it would grow on me, and I wouldn't be so freaked out.

I looked out the window to see we were turning down my driveway. He parked the Jeep and turned to look at me.

"You know what I'm going to say, but I'll say it anyway. You can't, under any circumstances, tell anyone about me."

"I promise," I extended my hand, pinkie finger poised and ready. He looked at in confusion for a second before chuckling. With a wry shake of his head, he linked our pinkies. I felt the familiar jolt. It made me want to curl up against him and burrow my face in his neck.

"Good." He followed me out of the Jeep and walked me to the front door.

"I have to ask something, though." I paused with my hand on the knob.

"I'll answer if I can."

I frowned at his odd response before diving in. "The first time I met you, you needed crutches to get around. Now, suddenly, you don't need them anymore. What happened?"

Drake winced. "I really...ask me that later, okay? I promise to give you answers."

"Why?"

"Because...you might look at me differently once you know the truth."

"And I don't look at you differently now?" I raised an eyebrow as sarcasm dripped from my tongue. He smirked, shoving his hands into his front pockets.

"True, but this is a little different. Just trust I will tell you when the time's right. Okay?"

I glared up at him for a second before I relented. "Fine, okay. I'll wait. Thanks for showing me your home. It was nice. What I saw of it at least."

This was the awkward doorstep conversation every girl dreaded. Even though we hadn't been on a date, it always felt strange to have a boy walk me to my door.

"Would you like to hang out tomorrow?" he surprised me by asking.

My mind screamed at me to say "no" and go inside. But, my heart seemed to have developed a mind of its own because I heard myself answer, "Um, sure, I guess. What did you have in mind?"

"I thought I could officially show you Market Square since we had to leave in a hurry last time. The UT drama department is doing an outdoor production of *Hamlet*."

"Oh, that sounds fun." *And very public. I can do public.*

"Okay, great. I'll pick you up around eleven."

"Sounds good." I knew I had a goofy grin on my face, but I was glad we were trying to move past the whole man-wolf thing. I wasn't sure I could go without him in my life in some form or fashion.

"I'll see you tomorrow, then," he waved before jogging back to his car.

I let myself into the house and plopped onto my mattress as soon as I entered my room. The long way down reminded me I needed to break down and finally put my bed together. One day I was going to miss the mattress completely and end up slamming down onto the floor. It was a concussion waiting to happen.

❦ 15 ❦

❧

Drake

CALL ME A GIRL, BUT I LIKED THAT PERIOD IN THE MORNING just before the sun came up. Nothing was awake. Silence rules the land. I stared up at the cloudy black sky from my vantage point on the roof of the cabin. Sleep never came. My mind picked apart each conversation I had with Star, looking at it from every possible angle. My fear was that somewhere I'd jacked up the whole situation, and she'd leave.

Her terrified green eyes constantly flashed in my mind, making it difficult to breathe. Every thought that raced through her brain after she learned the truth sliced through me, breaking me down to nothing. My heart felt like it'd bled out on the floor at her feet.

"Drake. Phone call," Meliena broke into my thoughts as she walked across the roof with my phone in her hand.

I wanted to tell her I wasn't up for talking to anyone, but the only person I knew who would think to call me for anything was Star. It was too early for her to be calling.

I grabbed the phone from Meliena and motioned her to leave. "Something wrong?" I asked.

"Huh? Oh, um, no. I just couldn't sleep. Needed to apologize to you." My chest constricted at the insecurity in her voice.

"For what?" If anyone should be apologizing, it was me.

"I didn't handle the news well, Drake. Actually, I effed it up big time. I know you're not a monster."

I felt my chest relax as a smile spread on my face. "It's okay."

"No, it's not. I've always prided myself on being an open-minded individual, never stereotyping anyone, but I did just that. So, I'm sorry."

"All is forgiven."

I heard her deep, relieved sigh and had to chuckle. Damn, she was adorable.

I could hear her thoughts firing rapidly as she internally debated over whether she should ask me something. Rather than just telling her what she wanted to know, I waited, letting her work it out for herself. Finally, she spoke. "There's another reason why I called."

Oddly enough, state capitals were running through her mind.

"What's that?"

"I can't shake this feeling that you...I don't know, you don't think you're good enough for me. Like, my being around you will hurt me somehow."

My heart clinched in my chest at her words. It was already happening. Her soul was connecting to mine. It wouldn't be long before she started sharing my abilities. Was that something I wanted for her?

"Drake, please let me in," she whispered.

I didn't deserve to have her. Listening to how hard she fought to preserve Clint's memory made me realize just how deeply her heart loved. She still missed him. I wasn't sure she'd ever stop. The grief would dull in time; however, a part of her that would always mourn his death, the part of her he took with him to the grave.

I wasn't good enough for that kind of love. I'd killed people. I screwed up everything I cared about. My parents and John were proof.

"You can see inside my head. Let me in yours. Just this once."

Right then and there, I knew I'd never be able to deny her anything.

I let out a deep breath I hadn't realized I was holding. "I mess things up, Star. Always have. The rational side of me says to leave you alone before you get too deep."

"What if that's not what I want?"

"Doesn't surprise me," I muttered.

"What's your story, Drake? How did you end up so isolated?"

No one knew my story. I made it a point to keep it that way. But, I'd apparently developed diarrhea of the mouth, because I heard myself starting from the beginning. "My father ran my mother and me out of the tribe when I was sixteen."

Damn, the bitter words my father spewed that day still stung.

"I'd gotten into trouble for hunting on a neighboring tribe's land without permission. My father was reprimanded in front of our tribe, putting his position as Alpha into question. He'd turned to me with venom in his eyes and publically disowned me. I took it like the man I wasn't, yet. Didn't flinch when he told me he regretted ever letting me be born."

I heard Star gasp but I couldn't stop. If I took a break, I'd never be able to finish.

"He broke my mother's heart that day. She defended me, but the great Black Warrior wouldn't have any of it. He told her if she loved me so much, she was free to go with me. With the support of the tribe's elders on his side, he forced us to take what little we were allowed and leave without saying 'goodbye' to anyone." I clinched my fist at the memory of my mother screaming, her face red and wet with tears as two warriors manually carried her off the land.

"With nowhere to go, she decided to beg her parents' tribe to take us in. They were reluctant because they were Bears, and I was a Wolf. But the mark of the Supreme Alpha appeared on my shoulder during my meeting with the elders."

What's a Supreme Alpha? I heard her think, but decided to save that for another time.

"Word came to us that on the day my father disowned us, a Mountain Lions attacked the tribe. No one survived. I never cried over my father's death. Served the bastard right for what he'd done to my mother." I spat each word out.

"The mark of the Supreme Alpha gave us immunity in the tribe, but with her mate no longer alive, my mother's strength left her. She died that winter. The Bears tried to convince me another shifter killed her, but I know she died from a broken heart. Despite the vile things my father did, she loved him."

Star shifted, and I knew she thought I was finished. Damn, but I wish I was.

"The night I found her dead behind our hut, I cradled her lifeless body in my arms and cried for what felt like hours. When the Elders came to bury her, I refused to let her go. It'd taken six men to pry her from my grip."

Even now, I could feel her cold, lifeless skin against my hot flesh.

"She'd fought for me, and I'd failed her when she needed me most."

All my life I had to deal with the mark of death on my soul. I tried to ignore it. I tried to believe I was just as worthy and capable of love as everyone else.

But I wasn't.

I couldn't let Star die like the others. My heart wasn't listening to the truth. It cried out for her. As I stared up into the nothingness of the pre-dawn listening to her soft cries on the phone, I couldn't take in a deep enough breath. I knew I wouldn't breathe right until I could touch her again. She was my reason for getting out of bed every morning. She was the reason I walked, the reason I breathed. She was my very existence.

And I was going to kill her.

"You were just a boy, Drake," she whispered finally.

A hot tear rolled down my face, pooling in my ear. I was so glad no one was around to witness my weakness. It wasn't fair, damn it! I wanted to mark her as mine. I wanted to kill anyone who even thought about looking at her. But I couldn't love her like that.

"I stayed with the tribe until the Helena incident. After that, I was on my own." I said it with as little emotion as possible.

Inside, I was freaking out. A world without Star's emerald green eyes or her heart-melting laughter was a world I didn't want to live in. It was the little things that made her special. The way she wasn't afraid to push my buttons; her dry sense of humor; her aversion to socialization; her loyalty; the way she accepted people just as they were; the way her eyes lit up when she saw me; how she looked at the world through a different lens; how she did what she wanted rather than what others expected her to do.

I loved everything about her.

"I know people say 'I'm sorry' during times like this, but I'm not. If you hadn't gone through that, we would've never met. So, I'm glad, Drake. Might make me selfish, but I am."

"Makes two of us," I chuckled, trying hard to get myself under control. "Get some sleep, Star. I'll be there to get you before you know it."

"Goodnight," she yawned, and then she was gone.

As the sun peeked over the horizon, birds started to chirp and a rooster crowed ten miles away. I stayed where I was on the roof until the sun was fully in the sky before I swung down into my window and got ready for my date with Star.

I had to see her. After our conversation, I was feeling completely exposed. In spite of all the harsh realities weighing down against me, I couldn't stay away from her.

On her porch step a little while later, I took my first deep breath the moment our eyes connected through the glass door.

"Hey," she smiled brightly as she opened the offensive barrier and stepped out to join me.

My eyes slowly took her in from top to bottom. All the saliva left my mouth.

She was wearing a green dress with some sort of lacy sleeves that stopped just below her elbows. The skirt on the dress wasn't very long, putting her amazing, creamy white legs on display. The belt she wore around her waist brought my attention to her chest. My eyes got stuck on that area as all thought left my brain.

Damn.

It was a good thing she couldn't read *my* thoughts or she'd know just how badly I wanted to push her up against the wall and kiss her.

"Wow, Star." It was all I could say. I couldn't verbalize what I really wanted to say ...yet.

I was growing uncomfortable. If I didn't get her off this porch and into my Jeep, I was going to be in big trouble.

Her cheeks pinked as she brushed her hands self-consciously down her dress. "I thought it was time to pull out some of my more colorful outfits."

"You always look beautiful, but this is definitely special." I struggled to keep my voice calm as I led her down the steps. I noticed she was wearing brown combat boots that looked like the ones I'd worn during World War I, but she had the sides and tongue of the shoes folded down, making them look floppy. Boots sometimes made girls looked shorter, but on her they only drew attention to the impressively firm muscles in her legs.

I struggled to think of something to say once we were in the Jeep. I was used to the Star in black hoodies, dark jeans that hugged her from waist to ankle, and black converse shoes. The woman sitting next to me was an entirely new creature. And she smelled way too good for my sanity.

The entire drive to Knoxville was made in silence. I helped her out of the SUV once I'd parked and slid my fingers through hers under the pretense of helping her down the narrow stairs of the parking garage. Even when we made it to the outdoor stage, I kept our hands linked. Her touch kept me calm and my more animalistic urges under control. We spread out the blanket I'd grabbed from the backseat, but when she moved to sit beside me, I pulled her down so that she sat between my legs and used my chest as a backrest.

Heaven.

I'd traveled all over the world and experienced a lot of things, but nothing came close to how amazing it felt to have her in my arms. The actors could've been totally naked having a full-on orgy on stage and I wouldn't know, because for two hours I watched the play through Star's eyes. The way they pooled with tears when Ophelia died. The anger that flared in them whenever Polonius made an appearance on stage. She was so expressive. I could only imagine how she would look in my arms for an entirely different... more intimate purpose.

Her thoughts were even more endearing. I was glad she'd stopped singing *Journey's* "Don't Stop Believing" in her head like she'd done the whole way over.

Hamlet's such a drama queen.
Ugh, that girl really needs to wear a bra with that costume.
I'm not sure I could pull off insanity like Hamlet.
Drake smells really good.
I wonder if he likes sitting like this.
I sort of hope the others never come. I like us.
I'm not sure I could die for love.

I couldn't help it. The way the sun radiated on her face, the way she bit her bottom lip when she concentrated, how she traced my arms around her waist was all too much. I gently cupped her chin, turning her head so I could claim her lips as mine. The first time I'd kissed her, she'd hesitated a few seconds. This time, she rested her head back on my shoulder and demanded more with her mouth.

So. Damn. Good.

She groaned as I cradled her head in my hand forcing myself to keep it there when what I really wanted to do was cop a feel.

A deep throat clearing brought me back to the present and I reluctantly released her.

She smiled up at me with glazed eyes. "Why'd you stop?"

"Because this isn't the place for what I want to do to you."

Her cheeks went adorably pink as she quickly turned her attention back to the stage. I chuckled as I placed a soft kiss in her hair. Another day, another time, I'd tell her she didn't have to worry about us sleeping together. But for now, I was content to soak up every uninterrupted second I had with her.

When the play ended and all the applause had been given, I reluctantly let Star go so we could both stand up.

"That was perfect." The smile Star flashed up at me was so bright I almost lost my balance as I bent over to retrieve our blanket. She wrapped her arms around my waist as I straightened and sighed. "Thank you so much for bringing me here."

I hugged her tightly against me, not wanting to let her go. When her stomach growled loudly, I laughed. "I think I need to feed you...now."

"Yeah, maybe. But I'm in the mood for something sweet and fruity," she buried her face in my chest like she was embarrassed. My heart melted a little more.

"There is this great place that serves Italian ice. Does that sound good?"

She pulled herself away from me and slid her hand through mine. "Lead the way, kind sir."

"Anything for you, my lady." I bowed as gallantly as I could. The giggles that bubbled from her as we made our way to the restaurant was totally worth the spectacle I probably made in front of hundreds of people.

Anything to make my girl happy.

I led her over to Rita's. Her eyes lit up as soon as we stepped inside the place. That little pink tongue of hers stuck out as she practically drooled over the Italian ice on display. It took her ten minutes to decide what she wanted. The girl behind the counter was clearly irritated, but the second she seemed to try to rush Star, I shot a warning glare. The girl would back down and make herself busy elsewhere. Finally, after tasting every flavor they had, Star ordered a cherry chocolate misto while I got sugar-free mango peach Italian ice.

"Do you want to eat it in here or walk around?" I asked her.

Her shoulders lifted and she was about to give her autopilot response of, "I don't care." However, at the last second, she changed her mind and said, "Let's walk."

As we walked in circles around the square, Star was silent, but not for lack of conversation. Rather, she was too busy inhaling her dessert to come up for air, let alone talk. Once we were finished, I grabbed her cup and tossed it in the trash receptacle along with mine.

"Come on, let's check out some of these places," I motioned to the first little shop we came to. Inside, Star went straight to work modeling wacky hats and sunglasses for me, and I let her dress me up in scarves and hair clips.

When she pulled out her phone to take a selfie, I grumbled my discomfort. "I'm not taking a picture wearing a bright pink scarf and a red flower in my hair."

She studied me for a second, gnawing on the inside of her cheek. Then she nodded. "You're right. Those colors definitely don't go together."

She left the clip in my hair but replaced the pink scarf with a tan and blue zigzag patterned scarf she kept calling chevron patterned, but it didn't look like any chevrons I'd ever seen.

"Star," I sighed.

"Humor me wolf boy," she rose up onto her toes and kissed me on the cheek before holding her cell phone out to snap the picture. Our heads naturally gravitated toward each other, and she gave a sassy grin, showing off the pink heart-shaped sunglasses and the large, floppy purple hat I was currently crushing. Just as she pressed the button, I made a petrified face. She looked at the picture and exploded with laughter.

"Come on, Drake. You can do better than that."

"Alright, alright. Redo," I conceded.

This time, when she went to take the picture, I grabbed her face and kissed her hard and fast. Her eyes sprung open the second I released her and tore off my girly getup.

"That's...hmm. Not sure I can post that," she muttered as she studied the picture.

"No one sees those pictures. Got that?" I warned. God, if the gang caught wind of them? I'd never hear the end of it.

"Don't get your panties in a twist. It's for my own guilty plea-sure," she winked before returning the items to their proper places. Then, grabbing my hand, she dragged me out of the store.

As we browsed through the other shops, taking hundreds (at least it felt like hundreds) of pictures. We talked about her days on the track team, argued over which indie band was better (I said *The Script*, she said *Mumford & Sons*, which I countered with the fact that they'd become too mainstream to be considered indie), and talked about our favorite writers.

Star surprised me with her obsession with books. The girl loved her Russian and Irish writers. She was also a huge Samuel Beckett fan, which I didn't expect. I pegged her for a Maya Angelo or Emily Dickenson groupie. When she claimed to be a huge lover of all things Poe, I had to draw the line.

"Poe is overrated," I rolled my eyes.

"What!? No way! Poe is one of the best writers America ever produced." She protested as she browsed a shelf of handmade greeting cards.

"Which is why American literature will never be as good as British literature. Poe had a standard MO with all his pieces. Sure, he changed it up a little bit here and there, but it was always the same. He was a pop fiction writer and usually too doped up to speak coherent sentences most of the time."

"You're right about British literature being better but wrong about Poe being a pop fiction writer. He delved into the corrup-tion of mankind and was a master of depicting the deep pain and longing for death that comes with losing someone you love. His work is morbidly beautiful." Star sighed as she leaned against my arm. I slid my arms around her waist, drawing her back up against my front. The second we made contact, my body relaxed.

"*Poe* and *beautiful* should never be used in the same sentence," I chuckled. "Trust me."

"You act like you knew him."

And this was where I found a clever way to avoid the subject. Unfortunately, with her so close to me, my brain short circuited. So, I dumbly responded with, "I'd rather not say."

"Oh, come on! You can't do that to me!" She broke our connection to look at a set of Russian nesting doll measuring cups.

"Do what?" I feigned ignorance, albeit not very good. I wasn't going to win an Oscar with this train-wreck performance.

"You can't tell me you *knew* someone who was a literary legend and not give me the details. It's like saying you were the only one who saw the worst car wreck in American history but refuse to give your testimony to the police." She wrapped her arm around my waist and nestled closer to me as we walked around a display of scarves made from recycled plastic bottles.

"Maybe I had to be silent for a reason. Maybe I caused the accident and didn't want to incriminate myself because my girl-friend would kill me." I stopped to mindlessly stare at a display of redneck wine glasses, also known as plastic solo cups super glued to a thick wine glass stem. *Did people really buy that shit?*

"Okay, newsflash, Poe's been dead for a pretty long time now. I think you're in the clear on this one."

I couldn't help but laugh at her persistence. She reminded me of an excited little kid.

"Trust me on this, baby. The less you know the better."

She was only silent for a few seconds before she switched the conversation.

"Have you ever been outside the country?"

Now I really felt like I was walking through a landmine. Even though her mind was pretty much an open book today, I still hadn't been able to pick up on how she felt about the whole legend thing. I didn't want to overwhelm her too much right out of the gate. But, if I ever had a chance in the fight for her heart, I had to tell as much of the truth as I was allowed whenever possible.

"Yes, I have."

"Really? What for? Where did you go?"

I looked around at all the people walking by and knew we were in the wrong place for this discussion. Instead of answering, I grabbed her hand and led her out of the store. "We'd better go somewhere else for this conversation."

Her frustrated huff definitely wasn't subtle. I had to bite my cheek to keep from laughing. Once we were back to my Jeep, I helped her into her side before climbing in on mine. I drove us down the interstate for a while with no particular destination in mind. Finally, when I felt we'd put enough distance between us and Downtown, I started talking.

"After Helena died, I went on a quest to find death. It was more of the guilt talking rather than the heartbreak. If I'd really been grieving over her, death would've come easy." I sighed, knowing my words were going to illicit more questions from her. Part of me wished I'd written a handbook for all this stuff in the event Helena's descendants came back. It would've made life so much easier now.

"If there was a war, I was in it. I put myself in harm's way and walked away unscathed every time. I watched my friends, good men, die for a cause they never fully understood. I was labeled as a weapon of mass destruction long before the first atom bomb was dropped. All I had to do was forge my records and no one asked questions. I demanded to be placed in the toughest, most strenuous divisions and was given metals and honors I didn't deserve."

Here was the part that would probably freak her out. "I've had live grenades go off in my hands, survived being shot multiple times in the chest, and my submarine sank in the icy northern Atlantic Ocean surrounded by icebergs. War took me to a lot of different places, but I can't say I ever had fun."

I waited for a response. Star's brain was completely static, like she was in shock or something. Finally, she asked softly, "How many wars have you been in?"

"Every battle the U.S. has ever been involved in, until Afghanistan."

"Why's that?"

"The age of capturing war on video made the risk of being discovered more dangerous. I got away with forging my records in Desert Storm because of the years separating it from Vietnam. The turnaround between Desert Storm and Afghanistan was too close. I could've easily been exposed if I crossed paths with the wrong people, like lifers who'd promoted to high-up positions since Desert Storm. Besides, I was sick of all the fighting. It's hard to make friends with guys, only to have them blown to pieces right in front of my face."

I want to hold his hand, but I don't know how he'll take it.

Her thought made me smile. Only Star would be worried about me after I'd dumped a load on her the size of Europe. I linked our fingers and rested our joined hands on my thigh.

"Were you on crutches because of some war injury?" She surprised me by asking.

"No," I said slowly. I really didn't want to go into full detail with her on this, but it was obvious she wasn't going to let up until I gave her something. "Just because I can't die doesn't mean I can't develop a physical deformity or have a medical problem."

"So, do you have MS or something?"

I gripped my free hand on my steering wheel and tried not to let myself feel the uneasiness trying to settle in. "Wolf shifters can only survive on meat that is freshly killed, which means I need to eat my food as soon as I kill it. Store-bought meat makes us anemic. The longer I'm that way, the weaker my muscles become until I'm nothing but a skeletal form of my former self. I turn into something resembling a puppy destined to one day become a mastiff." I smirked, letting her know I'd heard that particular thought run through her head a while back. The blush that flushed on her cheeks made me full-on smile.

"After I decided to leave the military life, I gave up hunting because a weak version of me wouldn't be tempted to fight again if the call arose. It also helped me stay clear of pack drama. My position as Supreme Alpha, even without an actual pack to lead, makes me a threat to other Alphas. So, my debilitated state killed two birds with one stone."

"What made you drop the charade?"

"It wasn't a charade, Star. Once a Wolf shifter gets to that stage, he's permanently crippled. The morning of the first day I met you, I woke up with full use of my legs."

"Did I have something to do with your healing?" She began drawing circles on my arm, causing a harsh shiver to surge through me.

"My theory is that when you came into town, my body healed itself because I'm destined to protect you. I couldn't do that without my muscles fully functioning."

"Why do you need to protect me?"

"Because there are people out there who want to put an end to the shifters. They believe the solution is to kill us. They've been waiting a long time for this day to come."

Star shivered against me. I lifted our joined hands and kissed hers. "Don't worry, I'm all better now."

"Was that why you were gone so much?"

"Partly. Some of it was that I had to develop my game plan on how to deal with whatever comes our way. The other, more urgent reason for being gone was my desperate need for a hunting spree and the only place I could hunt without getting into trouble is deep in the heart of the mountains."

"So, what do you eat?"

"Mostly deer and mountain lion and the occasional bear. I have to make sure before I attack that it's not a shifter."

"How can you tell?"

"We all put off a particular smell that alerts others of who we are. Regular animals don't put off any kind of special smell. If it smells like plain animal, it's safe to kill."

"Weird," Star muttered.

So, Drake is a guy who can turn into a wolf. He's over three centuries old. Yikes! Talk about robbing the cradle. He's fought in a bunch of wars. Wow! He made himself crippled...and then I show up and "It's a miracle!" There are people on this earth who can live forever. How is that even possible? Can they bottle that somehow? I'm the key to all this craziness, which I'll think about that later. Holy crap! There are people who want to kill me. Definitely doesn't give me warm, fuzzy feelings to think on that too much. I'm sleeping with a baseball bat by my bed from now on. Yeah, normal everyday teen drama...my butt!

I couldn't hold back a chuckle. As if a baseball bat would do any damage to a shifter who wanted her dead.

Star turned and slugged me hard...for a mortal girl. "Stay out of my head, wolf boy."

I tilted my head back and outright laughed at her sweet insult. "I can't, babe. Your mind is far too entertaining." No reason to tell her again that I couldn't keep out of her head if I tried. "A baseball bat won't help you in this case. But, I have you under constant protection. You're safe."

"You can't do that, Drake. You'll be no help to me if you're sleep-deprived."

"I have some friends who take shifts."

Star frowned as she turned to study me. I fought hard to keep my eyes trained on the road. Her green orbs were too mesmerizing. "I thought you said you were a loner."

"Being a lone Wolf just means I don't affiliate with a Wolf pack. It doesn't mean I lack friends or a pack I can turn to if need be."

"Do you really trust these friends? Things didn't look so secure to me when I was at your house yesterday."

I sighed as I turned off the exit that would take us to my house. "I trust everyone on my security detail. I have a pack promise you will be safe."

"I didn't feel too safe."

"They were grieving, Star. They couldn't hurt you unless they had my permission, which will never happen."

"Are all your friends wolves? Wolf shifters, I mean." Star wiggled in her seat, and her skirt moved high up on her thighs. It took everything in me to keep my eyes on the road.

"Not exactly."

She swatted my arm. "Don't get evasive on me now. Spill!"

I chuckled. "You're adorable."

"Puppies, kittens, and babies are adorable." She rolled her eyes.

Instead of giving her a comeback, I answered her question. "Most are Wolves. But, my closest friends are a coyote, a skunk, a raccoon, and a squirrel."

"You can't be serious! What do they do besides spray you, give you rabies, eat your pet cat, or horde nuts?" Star giggled.

"A skunk shifter's spray can melt the flesh off your bones. A Raccoon's bite puts you into a vegetative state from head to toe. Coyotes are master manipulators and can disorient an enemy long enough to make death feel beautiful. A squirrel shifter is really rare. Her fighting abilities can't be matched by anyone. Once a Squirrel is angry, she will fight until the death. She's fast as lightning, and her bite is deadly."

"Remind me to never piss your friends off," Star muttered under her breath.

"As long as you aren't permanently evil and refrain from trying to wage war against the shifters, you're safe. If you had my mark of the Supreme Alpha on you, you'd be safe for life."

"How does that happen?"

Just thinking about the ceremony made me burn in places I had no business burning at the moment. I cleared my throat, begging my vocal cords not to give out on me. "It's something that happens when the Supreme Alpha consummates with his mate."

"Oh."

Star's mind flashed to a dimly lit room. Heavy panting bounced off the walls as two sweaty figures came into focus. It took me a second to realize the couple clinging to each other was Star and I.

Her nails dug into my bare back as she cried out. It took my addled brain another few seconds to realize she was having a fantasy of us together.

Oh, shit!

The Jeep swerved off the road, jerking me back to reality. I quickly regained control of the wheel, but my body had definitely gone haywire. I struggled to regulate my quick, shallow breaths, but my mind kept flashing to her fantasy.

I glanced at Star in my peripheral to see her face beet red. She knew I'd seen her thoughts. The tension in the Jeep grew in mammoth proportions as I continued to drive, desperately trying to get my body to stand down.

"So, um, how were shifters created?" Star squeaked out a diversion.

"The Creator," I sighed, gladly taking her offer. "We sort of started out as a form of angels on earth. He gave us the ability to turn into animals so humans wouldn't be able to detect who we were. When the serpent broke rank and turned evil, causing Adam and Even to be thrown out of Eden, all the shifters were punished. We became morphing humans instead of morphing angels, and we were given a type of immortality."

"What does that mean?"

"If we follow the rules and protect what we were created to protect, we can decide when it's our time to go. We have to report to Destiny, or someone with the authority to speak to her, who in turn delivers the request to the Creator. If He thinks we've served our purpose, we can go to Heaven. If He still has plans for us on earth, He denies the request."

Star snorted. "That's a bunch of spiritual hogwash."

I glowered at the road. "So, you can accept that there are immortal humans who can change into animals who roam the earth, but you can't accept the existence of a Creator and His involvement in creation?"

"I just don't see how He would care about us that much."

"Trust me, He cares."

"If He cared, He wouldn't have let Clint die."

And so we finally came to the barrier between her and the Creator. "Star, just because Clint died doesn't mean the Creator didn't care about him. It was Clint's destiny to die because his death served a greater purpose. A purpose we may never know or understand."

Star shivered hard as she squeezed my hand, as if she needed the reminder we were both still alive. "Change of subject. Where are we going?"

"I thought we'd finish the day going for a nice run. Get your legs working again."

Star let out a snort of laughter. "As if! I'm not running. In case you haven't noticed, I'm not exactly dressed for it." She ran her hands over her dress.

"As interesting as it would be to see you run in that, I had your mom pack your gym bag." I pulled it up from the backseat where Mrs. Allistar stored it last night when I dropped Star off. I'd called ahead so she could slip it in while we were talking on the front porch.

"I'm going to kill her," Star mumbled under her breath.

16

Star

"God, I'm really going to kill her." I could barely breathe as I struggled to keep up with Drake.

I wasn't just a little out of shape. I was *completely* out of shape. After running only half a mile, my lungs burned and I wheezed with every breath I took. Two miles into the run, I was sure I was going to die from an exploding heart. The cool air got trapped in my lungs, the flab on my legs itched from all the jiggling, and my bladder was really starting to feel the Italian ice. Unable to take another step, I came to an abrupt halt and doubled over to try to get rid of the annoying runner's cramp in my side.

"Can't. Breathe. Need. Water. Gotta. Pee." I rasped. I glanced up through bleary eyes to see his smiling, unfazed face. Jerk.

"This is seriously unfair," I said in disgust.

"Come on. It's not *that* bad." Drake rolled his eyes, but I saw his teasing smirk. I was going to pay him back some way, somehow when he least expected it.

"Shut up, wolf boy." I shoved at him. He didn't even have the courtesy to pretend I'd used enough force to knock him off balance.

"Last person to the bathrooms has to pay for dinner," I said and took off running, praying my bladder would hold, too occupied to notice he'd given me a ten-second head start. Even with the handicap, he still had to slow his pace to lose.

What a hollow victory.

17

Star

"I HAVE A QUESTION FOR YOU," I SAID ON THE PHONE A WEEK later.

"Okay. Give it to me." I liked that Drake played along even though he already knew what I was going to say.

"Does your feud between you and Sam run deeper than just a fight over a girl?"

"Sort of. It's complicated," he sighed loudly.

"Well, could you uncomplicate it for me?"

When he was silent for more than a minute, I began to think he wasn't going to say anything else. But, before I could come up with a topic changer, he said, "Sam's tribe had problems with Wolves before they ever adopted me. I never got the full story, but it was mostly a power issue. They didn't like that the Wolves carried on the Supreme Alpha line. And if I had to guess, the Wolves were cocky about it, too."

"So, if your mom was a Bear, how are you a Wolf?" I rolled over onto my back and stared up at my motionless ceiling fan.

"My father was a Wolf. The wife takes on her husband's form when she marries."

"So, she became a Wolf which meant you would be one, too."

"Sort of. The Bear tribe believes the Bear gene can be passed down from the father to the daughter and the daughter to the son without the daughter being directly affected. Which, if correct, would mean I'd turn into a Bear, not a Wolf. I did neither. I'm actually a hybrid of the two. I'm much larger and stronger than the average Wolf thanks to the Bear, but I still take on the full Wolf form."

"I'm glad for that. Could you imagine having the nose, ears, feet, and tail of a wolf and the head, eyes, and body of a bear? You'd be one scary looking beast. No offense."

His soft chuckle washed over me and made me wish we were talking in person. It was weird. When I wasn't around him, the grief over Clint was alive and present, but the second I touched Drake, all the pain was gone and in its place was a longing I was too young to understand.

"None taken."

"Guess what I did today." I flopped back onto my stomach and looked around at my fully-decorated room. It was time for a change of subject.

"You finally unpacked your things."

Well, apparently he wasn't going to be nice and play along this time. "Not fair, wolf boy."

"Why wolf *boy*? I'm a wolf *man*, baby." His voice dropped on the word "man." Talk about a loaded ego.

It felt good to flirt a little. I was terrible at it, but he was being nice. His voice, his presence was healing me. I felt it every morning when I climbed out of bed. Instead of dreading another day, I looked forward to seeing Drake. He'd begun picking me up every morning and held my hand every chance he got. I knew I was developing somewhat of an addiction to him. But, I wasn't ready to go through a twelve-step program to get him out of my system.

"Someone is here for you," Dad said as he poked his head into my room.

"Hey, can I call you back later?" I asked Drake.

"I'll be eagerly waiting for your call."

I was glad he couldn't see my red face as I hung up and walked into the living room. Wayley and Onyx were listening to Mom as she explained the importance of every figurine in her glass cabinet. Poor souls. Mom could go on for hours about her knickknacks.

"Hey guys. What's up?" I asked, trying to save them.

"Hey, Star. We just wanted to see if you were up for going ice skating." It was Onyx who spoke. Wayley seemed genuinely interested in the ceramic dust collectors.

I bit my lip. Me on solid ground was dangerous. I could hardly fathom what it would be like if I was on ice in a pair of skates.

"You could invite Drake. It would be fun," Mom encouraged.

Wayley and Onyx smirked at each other. I knew they'd seen the two of us together at school, but since he didn't always eat lunch with us, I hadn't been forced to address the "Drake issue" with the group...yet. Not even after the movie.

"We're not an item," I informed everyone in the room. It was the partial truth. We hadn't had the "define the relationship" talk...yet.

"You could ask him anyway. It would even out the group," Wayley ignored my comment. The twinkle in her blue eyes told me I wasn't fooling anyone.

"Please, it'd be so much fun." Onyx gave me a pouty face.

I still didn't like being sociable, but they were growing on me.

"Okay," I sighed, giving in way too easily for my comfort.

"Great, we leave in an hour!" Wayley clapped her hands.

I went back into my room, pulled on a pair of faded skinny jeans, a gray thermal shirt, my favorite navy blue surplus jacket, and my black fold-over boots before calling Drake.

"No," he answered instead of his usual "hey, baby."

"Please. You can't make me do this alone. I'll kill myself on those things." I begged as I cradled the phone between my ear and shoulder so I could pull my hair back into a messy ponytail.

There was a long pause, too long.

"Hello, you still there?" I asked. Maybe we'd lost signal.

"Yeah, I'm here. I don't know how much I'll be able to keep you safe when I'm also flailing around."

"Please, Drake. I'll repay you somehow. Pleeeeeeease."

His deep sigh told me I'd won. "Fine, but only for you. And we're *not* riding with Chris and Giles. One wrong look at you and they lose a limb."

"Deal. Come as soon as you can. They're leaving in about an hour."

"On my way."

I closed my phone and walked into the living room where Onyx and Wayley had parked themselves on the sofa.

"Is he coming?" Onyx asked.

"Yes, but we're taking a separate car."

"That's probably for the best. My car only fits five miserably." Onyx scrunched up her nose like she'd smelled something funky.

I joined them on the sofa and secretly willed Drake to break every speed limit as the girls talked about boys and how much they hoped to have boyfriends, or at least dates, for prom. I didn't say much. Prom was overrated; just girls' playing "pretend wedding" and guys attempting to get into said delusional girls' pants. I heard the doorbell ring and jumped up with relief, beating Mom to the door.

Thank you I said silently, and he flashed his sexy dimple showing.

"Hey, Drake. Great solo yesterday." Onyx smiled as we walked into the living room holding hands. No matter where we went or what we were doing, he had to hold my hand. I wondered if it was like a security blanket for him.

"Oh, that was supposed to happen? I thought the band forgot to play." I blushed at my admission. Could I be any more of a dork?

Drake only chuckled and sat down in the recliner. Because the couch really only sat two people comfortably, I took the armrest of the recliner and tried not to focus on how close we were.

"Oh, that must be the guys. I think we can go," Onyx jumped up and answered her buzzing phone.

Drake and I stood at the same time, and he surprised me by pulling me against his chest and whispering into my ear, "You look beautiful."

A strong electric current shot through me as I struggled not to blush. He released me only to link our hands together again. Wayley looked at us over her shoulder and smirked. I turned to stare at the empty wall to avoid her.

Drake led me to his Jeep, and together we followed Onyx's tiny car over to the school where Giles and Chris were waiting. They eyed the Jeep, and I felt him tense beside me.

Down, boy. It came to my mind before I could stop it, and he let out a bark of laughter.

"Resorting to dog commands now?"

"No, that was completely accidental and not meant the way it sounded." I could feel the blush spreading up to my roots. God, I was screwing this up!

Drake chuckled and brought my hand to his lips. "It's okay. I got the message."

My knuckles tingled from where his warm lips touched them, and breathing became exceedingly difficult. "Um, why do you worry about Chris and Giles anyway?" I managed to ask.

"Because the Creator gives humans the freedom to choose. You may be drawn to me, but you have the power to reject me."

"Huh, interesting." Definitely didn't expect that one. "Well, in any case, you shouldn't worry about either of them. They're not my type."

"And what exactly is your *type*?" He gave me a heated glance.

Tall. Dark. And howls at the moon.

Drake squeezed my hand a little tighter, and I realized just what I'd admitted. My eyes darted over in his direction, but other than a slight tick in his jaw, he seemed completely unfazed.

I decided a change of subject was in order and ended up talking about books, our favorite topic, the entire drive to Ober Gatlinburg.

I liked that Drake had so much knowledge about literature. Clint was all about track and football. I'd come to dread Friday through Monday during football season. The wonderful thing about Drake? He was straight and hated professional sports. I. Was. In. Heaven!

When we arrived at Ober, everyone filed out of the vehicles and followed in groups of two inside the arena where fifties music crackled over an antiquated sound system. I reluctantly exchanged my shoes for a pair of white skates that had seen better days. Drake asked for the largest men's skate they had, which were still too small for his feet.

Once Giles and Chris realized Drake and I were *together* together, they paired with Onyx and Wayley. They took to the ice before we did, and I could hear the girls' delighted giggles.

"Are you ready to make a fool out of yourself?" I asked Drake.

He gave me a dirty look before wobbling on his feet. We scuffed our way onto the ice. I felt the blade of my right skate slide precariously and cringed. This was going to be painful. Once I was completely on the ice, I clung to the handrail and turned to look at Drake. He latched onto my hand and muttered, "Don't you dare let go."

We made it four strides before our first epic crash. Drake managed to maneuver us as we went down so his back slammed onto the frozen ground, and I landed on top of him. Of course, without an ounce of body fat, he wasn't exactly the most comfortable surface to smack face-first into.

You need some meat on you, wolf boy.

"You don't want me soft, baby," he answered out loud.

I used his concrete chest as leverage to stand up instead of responding to *that* comment. I was beginning to like the silent communication thing. Clint and I always tried to have it, but he was usually thinking about food when I was thinking about snuggling up on the couch to watch a chick flick.

We took a few more strides before my feet came out from under me. Drake yanked me in an attempt to compensate, and I ended up face-planting into his chest...again. At least he smelled really good. I'll admit I might have taken a longer sniff than was appropriate. It was all the darn Wolf dreams I'd been having lately. Knowing Drake really was a Wolf hadn't helped my overactive imagination at all.

Once I found my balance, he let me go but kept our hands connected. Despite the cold, I was warm thanks to him. He must have some sort of built-in space heater or something because his body was freakishly warm every time we collided into each other.

Onyx and Giles lapped us, and she looked back to give me a wink. I heard Wayley scream and turned to see her and Chris in a heap, both laughing.

Drake muttered something and wobbled. I assumed it was a curse because he began to topple forward. I tried to right him, but he was too big. He crashed first and I fell second.

"Ugh, sorry," I grunted as I tried to pull myself off him.

I made the mistake of looking into those silver blue eyes and suddenly the world around me ceased to exist. All I could think about was how close we were and how warm he was and how ruggedly beautiful he was...and how much I wanted him to erase the few inches between us and kiss me.

I held my breath as he brought me closer. Slowly, he reached up and buried his fingers in my hair. My limbs were shaking as I watched his eyes darken.

"You're so beautiful," he whispered, his hot, spearmint-scented breath caressed my face.

He studied me intently, as if he was fighting some internal conflict and my face contained the answer. Our lips meshed and I closed my eyes as my heart began to river dance against my ribcage.

His tongue immediately slid past the barrier of my lips, and I sighed, drinking in his taste. I should've been embarrassed to be kissing him on an ice skating rink with people all around us, but I wasn't. In fact, time and space ceased to exist. All I could feel was him and his hands sliding down to my hips. More. I needed so much more. Freezing cold ice shavings splashed onto my face, scaring the crap out of me.

"What the heck?" I tore my lips from Drake's and glared up at the invader only to find Giles's goofy grin.

"Keep it G-rated, ladies," he smirked before skating away to rejoin Onyx.

"Idiot," Drake growled loud enough for me to hear.

"It's okay. Perfect timing, actually." I laughed nervously as I inwardly struggled to calm my hormones down. Someone had released a flock of bats throughout my body, causing all my muscles to spasm from adrenaline.

It took us both several tries before we could stand again. I didn't know about him, but that kiss had turned my legs into mush.

"I've come up with so many ways you're going to repay me for this," he muttered through clenched teeth.

"Oh, but this is payback for that little surprise run you planned last week. You remember? The one where you laughed at my pain and misery," I glowered up at him accusingly. "Besides, you know you're enjoying this," I smirked just before I plopped down unexpectedly onto my behind.

"Why didn't you try to catch me?" I asked, stunned that he was still standing.

"You were getting too confident." He tried to shoot me a glare, but I saw the glint of humor in his silver eyes.

Drake helped me up, and we skated a few more strides, triumphant in our first completed lap around the rink. Neither of us talked about the kiss, as usual. But then again, what could either of us say? I wasn't sorry and neither was he. It was more accurate to say neither of us tried to pick up where we'd been before Giles interrupted us. That was the down side of going on a group date. There was never a moment of privacy.

I would like to say it got better from there, but we spent more time trying to pick ourselves up off the ice than we did any actual skating. Finally, my body had enough.

"Let's take a break," I gasped after an exceptionally painful fall. Despite his best efforts, Drake couldn't always prevent me from crashing onto the ice.

He helped me to solid ground, and we both plopped down onto the nearest bench.

"I think we should stick to dry land from now on," I said between gulps of air.

"Sounds like a plan," he nodded, barely winded. His hand still clutched mine. I wanted to move it to run my fingers through my disheveled hair, but his grip tightened, anticipating my thoughts. So, I happily left it where it was. If he was fine with me looking like the bride of Frankenstein, then so was I.

"Let's return these death traps and get some hot chocolate." I offered.

Before I could really fathom what he was doing, he dropped down onto his knees and unlaced my boots. I felt like Cinderella, only instead of the prince putting my shoe on, he was taking it off. He carried both sets of boots in one hand while keeping my fingers locked in his other as he toted us over to the skate return. I slid my numb feet into my combat boots and began to shiver uncontrollably. He didn't seem fazed by the sub-zero*ish* temperature of the rink.

On our way over to the concessions stand, Drake stopped by a booth and bought a pair of emerald green gloves with a matching toboggan.

"Put these on," he said as he tore the plastic away and turned to face me.

"Green?" I eyed the gloves.

"It reminded me of grass, like your eyes." he answered as he shoved the gloves over my hands and plopped the toboggan on my head.

"Thank you?" I tilted my head to the side. No one had ever likened my eyes to grass before. I was jointly flattered and offended.

He took my hand into his, and we continued on our quest for hot chocolate. Well, at least I was in search of hot chocolate. We finally found the booth, and he bought me my scalding, chocolatey goodness but only ordered ice water for himself. We sat down at a round table beside the rink and watched Onyx, Giles, Wayley, and Chris twirl and tumble around the rink.

"I think those gloves would look good with your natural hair color." Drake surprised me by saying.

"How do you know I'm not originally this dark?"

"Wayley was thinking it today. She said she thought you were pretty and *it was a shame you hid red hair under such drabby black*." His voice went falsetto as he did a poor impersonation of Wayley. I couldn't help but giggle. "I'm quoting her on that, by the way."

"Well, I'm not sure if I'm ready to part with my black hair. It's kind of grown on me." I shrugged.

"I personally don't care what color your hair is. Just making an observation."

"Can I ask you something?" I turned to look at him. His thick hair was pulled back into a short ponytail nub, but one chunk had fallen free that he'd tucked behind his ear.

He nodded.

"Why don't you wear your hair super long? Doesn't that mean you are in mourning or believe you lost your soul? Something like that?"

He nodded again. "Something like that."

Please, you know about Clint.

He sighed. "Well, before Helena, my hair was really long. Made transformations much more painful. When she died, I decided I wanted to separate myself from my heritage. I cut my hair and left the tribal life for good. Unfortunately, I'm stuck with these eyes."

I straightened in my chair. "I like your eyes! What's wrong with them?"

Drake sighed as he raked his fingers through his hair, pulling the ponytail out in the process. The black, silky mass fell around his face, making him look disheveled...and mouthwatering.

"Wolves identify rank by the color of each other's eyes. Silver signifies the Supreme Alpha. Gold represents a general pack Alpha. And so on. I can hide the tat but the eyes don't lie."

"Why would you want to hide them?"

Because seriously, if you knew what those eyes did to me...

Drake smirked, reminding me I no longer had any secrets. Dang it!

"I just don't like how my eyes make other shifters treat me differently."

"So, what makes a Supreme Alpha different from a general pack Alpha?" I don't know why I hadn't asked before now. Every time he brought it up, somehow my mind went to something else.

"This really isn't the place for that discussion." Drake glanced around at the people walking by us.

"Couldn't you be cryptic?"

"Not without confusing the hell out of you."

I stared out at the ice, biting my lip as I tried to mentally go over what I'd read about the shifters in my book. Maybe the answer was hidden somewhere in all that material.

"You're not going to rest until I give you something, are you?" Drake sighed.

"Nope." I smiled proudly.

"Fine, you have your General of the Army. Top dog. Five star. That's the Creator," Drake raised his hand up above his head. "Then you have the Generals. Four Star badasses. Those are the archangels." He dropped his hand to about ear level. "The Lieutenant Generals. Three Stars. That's reserved for Destiny." He dropped his hand to chin level. "Major General is next. Two Stars. That's the Supremes." He lowered his hand to chest level. "Alphas are like Brigadier Generals. One Stars. Deserve recognition and respect, but unlike the in military, in my world, they can't talk to anyone higher than me while I can go all the way to the Five-Star Man himself if I needed."

"Cool. So, have you ever talked to the Creator?" I wasn't sure if I really wanted the answer.

"Only in my prayers like everyone else. I've never communicated with anyone with a higher status than Destiny. I haven't been the most willing Supreme in history."

"You've gotta admit, all this is pretty great."

Drake grinned. I couldn't contain my fascination. It was like reading a book and then suddenly meeting the main character in real life.

"Ready to get something to eat?" Onyx asked. I hadn't noticed they'd left the rink. I hoped she hadn't heard anything unusual.

"Um, sure," I nodded even though I wasn't hungry.

Drake stood and helped me onto my feet. My calves screamed in protest, reminding me I needed to start working out again.

We filed out of the skating rink and into our respective vehicles. Drake reached over and tugged off my glove before holding onto my hand. We rode in silence as soft music played in the background. Even though I knew my body was going to be yelling at me for days from all the falls I took, I'd had fun with him.

We stopped at a burger joint, and Drake and I both ordered salads. I was afraid of what bringing chicken or a hamburger into his car would do. I was adjusting to the idea of Drake being a Wolf shifter, but I wasn't ready to *see* Drake turn into a Wolf. And if cooked meat made him sick, I couldn't help but wonder if sickness was different for shifters than it was for humans. Like, were they stuck in one form or another until the illness was gone, or did they barf like the rest of us?

Onyx dropped the boys off at the school because Chris had some sort of athletic practice. I felt slightly guilty that I never paid much attention to him. I may not be interested in him, but he was a friend, and friends kept tabs on each other. We followed Onyx into my neighborhood, but instead of turning into my driveway, Drake went in the direction of the woods.

"Where are we going?"

Once we were hidden behind the tree line, he threw the Jeep in park and turned to smile at me.

"I'm not ready to take you home just yet."

"What did you have in mind?" I asked as I stared blankly into the woods.

Sitting in the woods like this, experiencing the nerves fighting in my stomach...it reminded me too much of Clint. My chest constricted as reality finally sank in.

Clint and I would never do this again, because he was gone.

Someone was wheezing, but I couldn't break away from my grief to see who it was. Something warm and comforting massaged my shoulders, slowly bringing me back to enough reality to make me realize someone was talking.

"Cry. Get mad at him. It's not okay, but it will be."

Strange words.

A few seconds later, it dawned on me that the wheezing was actually high-pitched sobs coming from me, and I'd lost my ability to breathe.

It wasn't fair! Clint died before we could resolve our issues! We never got to make up or break up. He just died! Coward! I hated him. I hated what he put me through. I hated that because of him, I was now broken beyond repair.

At some point, Drake pulled me into his lap and rocked me as I pounded my tiny fists into his solid chest. He took each blow without protest, not once getting mad at me for crying over another guy, a guy who once owned my heart.

Once the tears subsided, I felt a weight lift off my shoulders. I knew I wasn't in the clear. It was going to take more than a few dates with a guy I was seriously starting to fall in like with to let go of Clint, but I was ready to try.

"Sorry," I sniffed and wiped my nose with the sleeve of my jacket.

"Nothing to be sorry about."

His chin rested on my head as I buried my face in his neck. Peace fused into my bones. I prayed I never had to leave his comforting arms. Pulling back slightly, I looked up into his warm silver eyes.

"Kiss me, please," I whispered. I needed him to anchor me back to earth. I needed to feel something other than the numbness that was threatening to settle inside me again.

Drake slid his fingers through my hair, tugging slightly so that I was forced to tilt my head back. I reached up to cup his cheek, suddenly fascinated at how translucent my skin looked up against his naturally tanned skin. But the time for thinking ended the second he fused our lips together. His tongue plunged into the depths of my mouth, taking me under to a place where all I could do was feel my need and desire for him. My hands moved to clutch onto the front of his shirt as I shifted so that I was straddling him and our chests were meshed together. His large hands clamped onto my hips, pressing me down.

A gasp exploded from my lungs as stars blurred my vision.

"Damn, you taste too good," he groaned as he trailed kisses along my jaw line and down my throat. Right where my neck met my shoulder, he sucked hard, and I jerked against him.

Before I could tell him I needed more, one of his hands was on the move, stopping on my rib cage just below my bra line.

I whimpered, silently begging him slide on up for a feel. When he made no further moves, I picked his hand up and placed it right where I wanted it, crying out as soon as he made contact.

"God, you're so responsive," he growled against my neck before he began to lick behind my ear.

I'm pretty sure I purred as my hands developed a mind of their own, sliding down the front of his shirt to slip under the hem and grope his abs. When my fingers brushed along the waistline of his jeans, he hissed and bucked his hips.

He began to massage the tops of my thighs, inching closer and closer to where I needed him to be. For the first time ever, I regretted wearing jeans. But, there was an advantage to wearing jeans. If you know what I mean

Drake consumed my mouth and for a second I could've sworn I could read his mind.

Mine.

The voice was deeper, dominant, and I had the insane urge to bare my neck to him.

His fingers move to the button of my jeans, and my body began to hum God, I needed this.

Suddenly, while he was in the process of tugging down my zipper, his body arched back and he let out a cry of pain.

"What? What's wrong?" I immediately snapped out of my lust-induced haze.

He groaned, digging his fingers hard into my thighs.

"Drake! What is it? What's happening?"

Oh God, what if he was having a seizure? What if he wasn't healed after all? What if my weight was hurting him?

I lunged over into the passenger seat as my body shook with fear. "Drake. Drake! Please, talk to me."

"Stay in the car," he groaned as he clamored for the door handle.

Before I could speak, he tumbled out. Right before my eyes, his entire body blurred as he fell onto all fours. Then, he charged through the trees and out of sight. I stared at the pile of shredded clothing, trying to come with the grips the fact that I'd seen him leave the Jeep as a human and run into the woods as a Wolf.

I sat motionless, not completely sure what was going on. When ten minutes went by with no signs of Drake, I pulled out my phone and played Tetris. Thirty minutes later, a loud thud on the side of my door scared the holy crap out of me. I dropped my phone on the floor as I spun my head to see the black Wolf staring at me through the window. His large head tilted toward the back seat.

I couldn't help but take the opportunity to stare at him. He was beautiful. His glossy black fur gleamed in the sunlight, making me want to bury my face in it. His silver eyes flashed with impatience as I took my fill until finally he swung his head toward the backseat again.

"Huh?" I frowned when he motioned for the third time, his nostrils flaring. I spun around to look behind me, my eyes landing on a large duffle bag.

Oh. Sorry.

I reached back and grabbed onto the bag, tugging it up into my lap. Without hesitating, I opened the door and held it out to him.

"Oh, er, hmm," I frowned as I belatedly remembered he currently had paws instead of hands. But, he surprised me by carefully clamping the bag's strap between his sharp teeth and walked behind the Jeep.

I knew if I really wanted to, I could adjust the mirrors just right so I could see a very naked Drake change into his spare clothes. But, something about that made me feel like a creeper, so I resisted temptation.

Okay, so maybe I did get a really, really quick glimpse of his tanned, toned backside. And maybe I happened to notice the bear tattoo on his upper right thigh next to his...ahum...right before it was guarded by black boxer briefs.

Drake swung the backdoor open and tossed his bag in before slamming it shut and opening the front door. Once inside, he hesitated a second, staring out at nothing. Then, with a shake of the head, he turned the key in the ignition, bringing the Jeep to life.

He drove me to my house in silence and walked me to my door. I mumbled a "thanks" and turned to go inside.

"There are some things you are better off not knowing," he warned.

"Yeah, too bad I can't keep anything from you." I didn't look at him when I said it. I just walked inside the house, leaving him standing on the porch alone.

This was by far the worst way to end a good date...ever.

❦ 18 ❧

❦

Drake

I PACED IN THE WOODS BEHIND STAR'S HOUSE AND LET MY MIND
go over the day's events. Skating went exactly how I knew it
would: me spending most of the time on my ass. But it was
completely worth it to see the smile on Star's face and hear her
sweet laughter. She had no idea how completely she held my heart
in the palm of her small, slender hands.

Our time in the Jeep just before Destiny summonsed me…just
thinking about it made me hard and uncomfortable.

However, just thinking about how close I'd come to shifting in
the car made my blood chill. The fear in Star's eyes as I fought
hard for control was permanently etched on my brain.

The meeting with the leader of the Guardians hadn't gone like
I'd hoped. Destiny wasn't known for making threats, but she
wasn't playing when she made it clear I had to obey or suffer the
consequences.

I closed my eyes and replayed the conversation for the hundredth time.

Destiny waited for me in a ring of sunlight at the heart of the woods. Her violet eyes studied me before I bowed my head in a sign of respect. She might not be the Creator, but she still held enough power to bring me to my knees if she wanted.

"Thank you for tearing yourself away from Star, Drake."

I lifted my head to look up at her. The wind picked up, making her long white hair shimmer under the sun's rays. She shifted and the diamonds on her celestial white dress winked at me. Anyone who was fortunate to see Destiny in person was floored by her otherworldly beauty. Yet, she was completely untouchable. No angel, human, or shifter was allowed to come within ten feet of her without turning into a pile of salt. So, I kept my distance

"I've received word that you and Star are getting along very well."

I nodded, knowing she wasn't really waiting for a response.

"I'd hoped Fate's little game with the three of you ended when Helena and Raphael died. It seems history is repeating itself again."

I sat back on my haunches as she looked deep into my eyes. "You love her. I can hear it in your heartbeat. What I have to say is going to be hard to accept."

My hackles rose, and I struggled to control my need to pace. I silently prayed she didn't continue. If she didn't speak, then I wouldn't be forced to obey.

"It's very important the legend ends with Star. She must make the right decision or the Guardians will *be eliminated. War is brewing in the shifters.* Shadowmen *is growing at an alarming rate. If Star takes too long, we won't have anyone left to fight."*

"I know," I finally spoke. "What do you need me to do?"

"Star can't pick you, Drake. If she does, there will be war. I'm ordering you to either change her heart about you, or stay away. If you can't obey, I'll force you away from her. Are we clear?"

My chest constricted at her words as the command sank into my veins. My heart stopped beating for a second as reality took root. Destiny had spoken. I wasn't the one.

"I'm giving you three weeks. Make her stop loving you or leave. It's your choice, but under no circumstances are you allowed to tell her about this meeting."

The world tilted on its axis, and I whimpered as I struggled not to collapse under the weight placed on my shoulders. I couldn't lose Star. She was my purpose in this life. I knew the others wouldn't get the same command. They'd swoop in, romance her off her feet, and she'd forget all about me.

A whine escaped from deep inside me as I lowered my head onto the ground in submission. It didn't matter what I wanted. The Creator had someone else for Star.

Hot tears slid down my face as I stared up at the moon peaking through the trees. It wasn't fair, damn it! If she wasn't the one for me, why did I feel like my soul was being ripped out of my chest?

I'd spent life trying to understand why the Creator kept me alive. Why He wanted me on this screwed up earth. Then Star came into the picture and suddenly everything made sense. I was put on this earth to love her. Everything I did, everything I was, everything I lived for was for her.

Every damn bit of it.

Yet, I had to stand back and watch someone else love her, someone else marry her, someone else raise children with her.

Being tied to a boulder and forced to live at the bottom of the Atlantic for the rest of my life sounded more appealing.

With an angry roar, I picked up a fallen log and tossed it as hard as I could. It crashed into two other trees, knocking them down, they all exploded into sawdust.

The wind shifted and I turned to see Bugsey walking toward me in her human form. She held a bag of pistachios to her chest as she nervously searched her surroundings before sitting down on a bed of dead leaves.

"What's wrong, Drake?" She whispered.

I sighed and ran my fingers through my hair. "Nothing you need to worry about."

"Word in the forest is Destiny paid you a visit."

Damn animals. They were worse gossips than old church biddies.

"Yeah." I let out a puff of air, mentally willing her to leave me alone. Unfortunately, I had a soft spot where Bugsey was concerned, so I kept my mouth shut and waited for her to say what she needed to say.

"Something's wrong, Drake. I can't explain it, but I can feel it. The squirrels say Destiny gave you an order: to turn Star away. Why would she do that?"

A thick knot formed in my throat as I struggled not to break down in front of her. "I'm not the one Star's supposed to end up with."

Bugsey frowned, dropping her bag of nuts. It shocked me that she didn't hurry to gather them up again. She just stared at me, confusion dominating her small, narrow face. "But, Drake, I...what does that mean?"

I studied the ground in front of me as I answered, "I have to remove myself from the equation or she'll do it for me."

Bugsey gasped as her eyes darted towards Star's darkened window. "But, but, why? If there is already love for you in Star's heart, there's *nothing* you can do to change it. And trust me, Star loves you. Last night during my shift I heard her talking in her sleep. She distinctly told the dream version of you she loved you. Why wouldn't you be the one?"

I shrugged, not sure what to say. Maybe the problem was Star made herself love me. It was possible she thought if she gave her heart to me, it would solve all our problems. If I wasn't such a selfish bastard, I'd leave her alone and let her mend so she could pick the right guy. But I was selfish, and until Destiny manually removed me, I wasn't leaving Star's side.

"Drake, something's not right. I know I just said that, but it's not. This isn't like Destiny at all. She's never made commands like this before. She usually handles things passive aggressively."

"Sometimes even supreme beings have to change their MO when the situation calls for it."

"Forget whatever Destiny said and listen to what your soul's saying. It will never steer you wrong."

"It already did once."

"No it didn't. I think if you searched deep within, you'd find you never really loved Helena. The only reason you were drawn to her was because one of her descendants would give birth to your soul mate. Nothing more."

If I listened to my heart, Star and I would be separated forever. Then what would be the point in living? But, God, I wanted her. I wanted to be able to wake up every morning with her in my arms. I wanted to know what it felt like to be connected to her so deeply we didn't know where I began and she ended. I wanted to see her round with my children. I wanted to grow old with her. I wanted us to make the cross-over from this life to Heaven...together.

"The Creator made us human, Drake, which means, like humans, we have the freedom to choose who we love in this life. It's not something designed by Destiny or Fate. It's a gift directly from Him. Don't fight your heart's choice. I know for a fact you'll never be happy without her."

Her mind flashed to a skinny guy with mousy brown hair and thick-rimmed glasses. She was sharing a jar of peanut butter with him as they laughed and talked. Then, it flashed to him driving away in a little beat-up Pontiac packed with all his worldly possessions.

"I let my own fears stop me from following my love across the country. I can't ever get that kind of love back, Drake. Don't do that to yourself. It hurts like crazy."

She picked up her nuts and gave me a gentle smile before walking away. I focused on Star's dark window. Could I take the chance of losing it all in hopes of gaining the only thing that mattered?

In the stillness of the night, I heard Star mutter in her sleep, "You're my air, Drake."

Four little words from her, and I had my answer: I'd do anything, be anything she needed as long as it meant I would be with Star.

God, forgive me, but I can't live without her.

❧ 19 ❧

❦

Star

I wanted to stay mad at him. It wasn't fair! He could invade my thoughts, yet I was completely clueless as to what went on in his mind. Unfortunately, I was drawn to him. He blamed it on the whole, "I'm designed to attract you" thing, but I was beginning to think a deeper force was at work. One neither he nor I could control. Exhibit A: the Monday after our group date, I found myself scouring the halls for him when it should be the other way around.

Silver blue eyes met mine, and I took my first deep breath since he left me on my front porch. He looked pissed, but I was still glad to see him.

"What are you doing in this hall? Don't you have Spanish?"

Obviously, he wasn't happy to see me. His eyes flashed with anger as his nostrils flared. His aggressive behavior completely ruffled my feathers. I wasn't sure how to respond at first.

"I just wanted to uh..." the words left my mouth. I knew we hadn't parted on friendly terms but still...

"Never mind," I turned around and stomped off.

He grabbed my arm and spun me around. "Nothing's wrong?"

I frowned, confused at his question. "Um, no. I just wanted to see you. To make sure we were still okay."

"That's it? You just wanted to see me?"

Why was it so hard for him to process?

"Yes."

Drake tugged on my hand, causing me to lose my balance and crash into him. Before I could take another breath, his hot, demanding mouth was on mine. Never had I kissed a guy at school. It was a hard limit for me. But at the moment, the building could be burning down and I wouldn't care.

His lips were bruising, but I gave back as good as I got, biting his bottom lip.

"Mmm, strawberry," he hummed against my lips. Our tongues dueled against each other, fighting for dominance.

He spun us so my back was up against a locker and his hard thigh was thrust between my legs. I sighed. So this was what it felt like to be consumed. God, never let it stop!

"I'm never going to get enough of you." Drake cradled my face as he eased back, placing quick, light kisses on my swollen lips.

"Alright, break it up!" A female voice commanded. We both turned our heads to see Mrs. Whitacre, one of the math teachers, shooting daggers at us with her small, beady eyes. If there was such thing as a rat shifter, she would fit the bill.

"Busted," Drake muttered under his breath as he put some space between us.

Before I could gather myself, he bent down to scoop up the books I didn't remember dropping and wrapped his arm around me.

"Better get to class before we get detention," he whispered in my ear. He tossed a wink at Mrs. Whitacre as we walked past her. Her cheeks pinked before she turned and scurried away.

Flirt.

The right side of his mouth tilted up slightly as he kept his eyes trained on the hallway in front of us.

Thank God my head by the time we were standing in front of the door to my Spanish classroom.

"I've got some things I have to do after school, but I'll call you." He kissed my forehead.

"Are you going to be in Band?"

Because, in all seriousness, he was the only reason I hadn't dropped the class.

"Yeah, but I have to leave early."

"Oh, okay."

He hugged me, brushing his lips over the shell of my ear. "Get to class, baby."

And with that, I was spun around and thrust into the room. By the time I turned around to shoot him a glare, he was gone.

During class, my mind tried to process his odd behavior. In the matter of minutes he had gone from mad to making out with me in a crowded hallway. It was almost as if he'd been preparing himself for battle. Had he thought I'd sought him out to give him the "it's not you, it's me" speech?

In band, he seemed more like the Drake I was coming to know. I spent the entire class period staring openly at him while he snuck in quick glances when he wasn't playing. At one point, he even winked. I liked watching the muscles under his tanned skin flex as he effortlessly played whatever instrument he was standing behind...er in front...uh, you know what I mean. Regardless, he made playing percussion look sexy.

Ten minutes before the bell rang, Drake grabbed his bag and left. Right before the door closed behind him, he turned and gave me a pant-worthy grin. Of course, no panting actually happened, but the urge was there.

At home, I was impossible to deal with. Not because I was mad or depressed, but because I stalked my phone like a freakin' crazy person. Every time it chirped, beeped, or buzzed, I was on it.

When night rolled around and there was still no word from Drake, I started to worry. What if something had gone wrong?

Finally, I cracked and texted him. I didn't want to be *that* girlfriend, but I wasn't going to be able to sleep until I heard from him.

Me: Hey, everything okay?

Ten minutes went by. Nothing.

Thirty minutes went by. Nothing.

Two hours went by. Nothing.

I fell asleep with my phone clutched in my hand.

Unfortunately, my dreams weren't any better.

Drake and I stood on the edge of a pier, facing each other. Every time I tried to get near him, he would transform into a wolf and growl at me. I didn't understand. Determination turned into anguish with every failed attempt. Then, just when I'd given up, he lunged, forcing me to fall backwards, freefalling toward the water. Just before my body hit the surface, I woke up with tears streaming down my cheeks.

❧ 20 ☙

***

Drake

"I CHECKED WAYLEY'S HOUSE. OTHER THAN HER OBSESSION with Theo James, nothing looked suspicious," Stella updated me as I paced in my kitchen.

"Found a stack of dirty magazines under Giles's bed, but nothing incriminating." Bugsey blushed crimson red. I coughed to disguise my chuckle. Just the thought of sweet, innocent Bugsey looking at a centerfold of a naked girl was funny.

"Mack sent Gina to Chris's house. Apparently the kid needs to run for sainthood, according to Gina." I sighed as I ran my fingers through my hair. With nothing turning up, I was starting to believe it wasn't someone from Star's circle. If that was the case, our search parameter expanded exponentially.

"Drake, one of Mack's guys just called. Someone is trying to break into Star's house." Meliena barged into the room, her brown eyes wild and her braid whipping into her face.

"Shit," I growled, charging out the door. I changed in midair and charged into the woods. My eyes sharpened as I dug hard into the ground with each sprint. I was going to catch whoever it was and kill him for even trying to touch her.

Just before I exploded out into the clearing to Star's home, Mack and three others joined me. The Alpha glanced over at me as we stormed ahead.

Let's get this bastard, Mack grunted, nodding his head.

I get to rip off his head, I growled. I didn't have to give any orders. Two broke away, moving to the front while the others stayed in the tree line in case the idiot tried to make a run for it. I spotted the intruder hanging half-way out Star's window.

I dug in deep, picking up my speed. With a loud growl, I lunged, ramming my head into the person's side. The guy yelped as his body flung to the ground. I immediately sank my teeth into his neck, daring the prick to move.

Don't kill him just yet, Drake. He might be able to tell us who the leader is.

I looked into the guy's frightened hazel eyes as they darted between Mack and me. I didn't recognize him. Either he was good at keeping a low profile at school, or he was one of the college kids Liena had overheard. God, I wanted to end him off. The thought of him in Star's room while she slept peacefully made me see red. I wanted his carcass on a platter.

Drake. Mack barked, barely penetrating my rage-filled haze.

As much as I hated it, he was right. I needed answers, and between my special ops experience and Mack's years as a secret service agent, we would get this bastard to talk.

Get him out of my sight. I don't trust myself right now. I growled, releasing my prey and running off. I needed to get away until they were gone, then I was going to guard Star's window until the sun came up. As pissed as I was, I invited the chance to kill anyone who even looked at her home funny.

I heard Mack bark and glanced over my flank to see the asswipe trying to make a run for it. Two Wolves pounced on him while Mack applied force to the jerk's neck. The guy kicked around for a few seconds before going limp. I could still hear his heart beating so I knew he wasn't dead.

He was safe for now, but as soon as I got what I wanted out of him, his ass was mine.

Just before I reached the clearing, the wind picked up and the smell of lavender, vanilla, and hot need slammed into me. I tensed and tilted my head back as a howl erupted from my body.

Star was in heat.

I skidded to a halt and jerked around to see the other Wolves staring at Star's open window. Their tongues loped out as they started panting hard. I charged back to her house, sliding to a stop under her window, baring my teeth at the others.

She's mine.

They all whimpered as I let the Supreme take control of protecting his woman. They quickly grabbed the guy by his shirt collar and dragged him off into the woods. I marked the parameter of the home as a precaution in case any other shifters caught her scent and prepared myself for a long night.

One thing was abundantly clear: until Star completed her cycle I had to stay the hell away from her. As it was, I was a panting, agitated mess. My teeth ground together as I fought hard to keep myself from going in her room and sleeping with her.

It was going to be a damn long night.

21

❦

Star

I WOKE UP NEEDING AIR. I GRABBED MY COMFORTER TO KEEP ME warm and slipped out onto the patio. Curling up in my spot on the swing, I stared up at the starless sky.

I knew deep down loving Drake was impossible. He was a part of a different world, one I could never understand, no matter how hard I tried. He was a friend I desperately needed to help me get out of the emotional grave Clint buried me in.

A rustle in the woods alerted me I wasn't alone. I tore my gaze off the bleak sky to see a large, dark form break the horizon. As it came closer, I recognized it as the black Wolf: Drake.

Why haven't you returned my text?

He walked right up to me and placed his head in my lap. I sat motionless, not sure what to do. His silver eyes were trained on me, but they were filled with so much sorrow. Not a fan of animals, I surprised myself as I began rubbing his ear. His chest heaved with a long, contented sigh.

I'm sorry if I came off pushy. When you didn't call like you said you would, I freaked a little. Last time something happened to me like that, it didn't turn out so well for the other guy.

Even though he didn't verbally respond, I could almost feel his acceptance. He nudged my hand when my fingers stilled.

Sheesh, aren't you a little impatient?

I could've sworn he smiled. He backed away and latched onto my comforter with his teeth. I frowned, trying to understand what he wanted. Then, as if giving me an answer, he tugged hard enough to make me fall out of the swing.

What the heck?

He grunted, motioning to my opened window.

I feel like I'm talking to Lassie. You wanna go inside, boy?

He flashed his teeth at me in warning, but I saw no malice in his eyes. I walked over to the window and climbed in. He followed effortlessly, jumping onto my bed with his dirty paws. Had it been any other animal, he would've been put outside. But this was Drake.

I climbed onto the bed, spreading the comforter out over us. He burrowed himself against me, his eyes staring at the window like he was expecting someone to come in after us. I ran my fingers through his fur as I snuggled closer to him.

It's so easy to be with you, Drake. I couldn't stay away if I tried.

Drake ran his thick, slobbery tongue over my face, making me giggle.

Knock it off, wolf boy.

Even though he was being playful, I couldn't shake the tension radiating from him. It felt like he was bracing for impact. From what, I didn't know. Maybe one day he'd tell me. For now, I wanted to enjoy the moment.

Promise me we'll never go a day without speaking to each other, especially when we're mad.

His soft grunt was all the response I needed.

The next thing I remembered, my alarm was going off. I glared at the offensive phone, willing it to shut up with my mind. Then, last night's events came back to me, and I found myself jumping out of bed. The sooner I got to school, the sooner I would see Drake.

I hurried to get dressed and met Mom out in the kitchen.

"Let's go," I rushed.

"Now, not so fast. I'm not taking you to school today," she smirked. I finally looked at her, taking in the sight of her in her favorite cat sweater. God, I wanted to burn that thing.

"Dad? Okay. Dad! Let's go!" I needed to see Drake so I could ask him what last night had been all about.

"No, Drake called while you were getting dressed."

"Wipe that grin off your face, Mom. We're just friends."

"That's him," she giggled when the doorbell clanged throughout the house. You would think she was the one in high school.

I grabbed my bag and my jacket before opening the door. He was dressed in jeans and a thin blue long-sleeved shirt despite the frigid temperatures.

"Ready?" He gave me a tender smile as he held out his hand to me.

"Bye, Mom!" I called back and then followed him to his Jeep.

Before opening my door for me, Drake spun me around, cupping my face right before he took my breath away with a heated, possessive kiss. God, I was hopeless where this boy was concerned. All too soon, he released my lips, drawing me into his arms so he could bury his nose in my neck. He took in a deep sniff, his body relaxing with the action. "Mornin', baby. Did you sleep good?"

"Yeah, but it would've been nice to wake up with you." I sighed as I clung onto his waist.

"I didn't want to wake you, but when your folks started moving around, I knew it was my cue to leave. Not sure how you could explain an oversized Wolf sleeping in your bed."

"What was that all about, anyway? I mean, not that it wasn't nice, but why did it feel like you were...I don't know. It kind of felt like you were stuck like that."

"For another time."

"Ugh, here we go again!"

He only took my hand and squeezed it. I was glad we were on speaking terms again, but I was tired of him hedging with me. Didn't he trust me?

"Just trust me when I say you are safe, okay?"

Oh, sure, I'm supposed to trust you, but it's okay for you to not trust me. It doesn't work that way, buddy.

"Can you do something for me today?"

"What?"

"Try to organize something with Onyx and Wayley for Friday night."

"What, why?" I'd hoped he and I could do something together on Friday.

"Because, I need to be out of town, and I don't want to worry about you."

"Do you have cause to worry about me?"

He didn't answer. I let out something that resembled a growl and slammed my fist down on the door handle. Given my lack of strength, the dang thing hardly moved.

"Just promise me you'll do it."

"No, Drake, I'm not going to promise anything. I'm so sick of you telling me half-truths and leaving me in the dark because you somehow think you're doing what's best for me. Well, newsflash, the only thing you're doing is pissing me off!"

Drake swerved off to the side of the road and cut the engine. For several moments he stared out at nothing before finally turning to look at me. His hair was down and the tips were still damp from his morning shower. The smell of his soap, citrus and pine, swirled around me, making it hard for me to stay mad. His Adam's apple bobbed as he struggled internally with something.

He reached over the console and cupped my face in his large hands. All the air left my lungs as I fell headfirst into his penetrating gaze. His eyes lowered to my lips, making me lick them in anticipation.

Please, kiss me!

I needed this. I ached for that connection with him. Even my nuclei were crying out for him to bridge the tiny gap between our mouths and make me forget my name, let alone why I was ticked at him.

"I can't tell you why I have to leave, Star. You just have to accept it." His warm, minty breath spread across my face. I took in a deep breath, mesmerized by his nearness.

"Are you seeing someone else?" I hated how my voice squeaked. If he'd just kiss me already, I wouldn't be able to think up junk like that.

He released me and leaned back against his chair with a *thunk*. His shoulders slumped as he looked down at his hands clenching the steering wheel. "No, you're it for me."

So much for that kiss.

"Give me something. Please. I'm tired of being in the dark about everything."

Drake ran his fingers through his hair as he turned to look at me. "The reason why I was *stuck* like that last night? It's an Alpha thing."

"Huh?"

Pink tinged his tanned cheeks as he stared out his window. "When a female the Alpha desires to mate with is, ah…" he paused to clear his throat, "in heat, God, this is embarrassing." He let out a ragged breath, running his fingers through his hair…again. I was surprised he still had hair left as much as he'd been doing it for the past ten minutes.

"Drake?" I pressed on. Part of me thought I knew what he was trying to say, but I needed to hear the words.

"It's the Alpha's job to take care of his mate. At night the urges are stronger, making the need more…*potent* I guess is the right word. He can't rest until he's either mated with her or she is no longer in heat."

At first I wasn't following. Then, my eyes grew wide as realization dawned. "You mean *I* made you like that?" I could feel my cheeks flaming. God, this was beyond embarrassing. He'd been stuck as a Wolf because the Alpha in him needed to have sex with me because I was ovulating? Someone shoot me now!

"Like I said, I need you to be busy Friday night. It's hardest to resist the first and last nights. Don't ask why, 'cause I don't have an answer."

"Since I'm not a Wolf, how would, um, how could..." I trailed off, my mind unable to wrap itself around the concept.

"Nothing can happen until you're a Wolf, Star. That's why I have to keep my distance."

"Gottcha. Then fine, I'll make plans for Friday."

He cleared his throat before he re-started the car. "Thank you."

I spent the rest of the ride staring out the window, trying to come up with something to do. Every time I had an idea he would say, "No, not good enough" or "That can't be fun." I gave up trying to think with him and just enjoyed the short silence before he parked the Jeep in his usual spot in the back lot.

We walked inside holding hands. I expected us to split as soon as we made it to my locker, but he waited patiently while I stowed away my books and grabbed what I'd need for first period. He stayed with me until we stood beside the door to the chemistry lab.

He didn't say anything. Instead, he kissed me lightly on the lips before he turned and walked away. I took a second to appreciate the view of his backside before walking into the classroom. Wayley was already there waiting for me, and I decided to give her the chance to decide on what we should do.

"Hey Wayley, got any plans for Friday?" I asked as casually as I could despite the fact I didn't normally do this sort of thing.

"Well, actually, no. Got something in mind?" She perked up in her seat. It was the first time I noticed she'd become more subdued around me. Maybe I was rubbing off on her. That thought almost made me snort.

"I thought you, Onyx, and I could do something together."

"That sounds like fun. What were you thinking of doing?"

"I don't know. I was kind of hoping you'd have some ideas."

"Let me talk to Onyx. She's the planner. We'll come up with something."

Happy, Drake?

⚜

HE WASN'T IN BAND.

Coward!

I thought of a million different reasons for his absence but none of them seemed to fit. After class was over, I pulled out my phone, prepared to call my mom and ask for a ride when I spotted him leaning against a row of lockers near the back doors of the school.

Where have you been? I glared at him as I walked in his direction.

He straightened but offered no apologies.

I followed him out to his Jeep in silence. I tried to clear my mind and think about nothing. While I was struggling with my seatbelt, it dawned on me that thinking about nothing was still thinking about something because I was in the act of trying not think about anything. This whole mindreading thing was messing with my head.

He pulled into my driveway and shut off the engine.

"I know you want explanations," he said, not looking at me.

I settled for studying his strong profile. His hair was much shorter than it'd been this morning. He'd shaved the sides and left only a little bit on top. I missed his long hair.

I wasn't sure why, but his jeans and black hoodie seemed out of place. I'd gotten accustomed to his tight black shirts, I guess. My mind went back to our time on the swing. His Wolf form seemed to fit better than his human form. That realization made me sad.

"I want to be honest with you about everything, but you

already know too much as it is. I won't risk your life, Star." He glanced over at me. "You're too precious to me."

"If I might be in danger, don't you think I have the right to know so I'm not caught with my pants around my ankles?"

"You can't prepare for this. You'll be dead before you realize it." His tone was bleak, and his eyes went dim as he spoke.

Fear closed my throat, and I felt an anxiety attack creeping into my chest. "What about you? Couldn't you die because of this?"

"Possibly. Shifters can kill each other, but the Creator must allow it. If anyone else attacks me, I heal too quickly for their wounds to off me. Watch."

He pulled out a pocketknife from his back pocket and flipped out the blade. He slowly pressed the tip into his skin and dragged it from the crook of his elbow down to his wrist. I cried out at the sight of him inflicting pain on himself, but anything else I planned on saying never made it out into the open because I was stunned into silence. Although the metal originally made an incision, before he moved it another inch, the mark was gone. When he was finished, it looked like nothing had ever happened.

"So, will you ever die?"

"Yes, like I said before, when the Creator says it's my time."

"What does that mean?"

"I have to fulfill my purpose on earth before I can move on."

"Your time isn't up, is it?"

He chuckled, "No, but there for a while I thought it was."

"Is the Wolf pack causing your problems? Is that it?"

"No, this is far worse than an overprotective pack of wolves."

"Please tell me, Drake. I can't afford not to know."

"Star..." he didn't say anything else, but I saw it in his eyes. There was some force keeping him from telling me. No matter how much I begged, he couldn't let me in.

"I just hope you don't regret your silence. You say you care about me, but if you never let me into your heart, how can I ever give you mine?" I sighed and grabbed my bag to leave.

"Wait, just wait a minute. It seems like all we ever do is end on bad terms," he growled.

I clutched my bag to my chest as if it were a shield.

"I need you to understand I will never hurt you. I will destroy anyone or anything that tries to lay a hand on you. Do you understand me? You're safe with me."

"But you aren't always with me."

"I'm always closer than you think."

"That's such a cliché," I scoffed to hide the fact his words comforted me.

"It's the truth." He shrugged. "You should probably get inside. Your mom is peeping out the window."

"Honestly, they think I'm suicidal," I sighed and went to open the door.

"Grieving...yes...suicidal...no," he said, stopping my movements.

"Sometimes I wonder which is worse, being the one living or the one dead." I stared out at the field.

"The one still living, always."

I turned and looked into his understanding eyes and something clicked inside of me, as if the final puzzle piece fell into place. I wasn't sure what it was exactly because I was still trying to see the whole picture, but I knew at that moment something changed inside of me where Drake was concerned.

"Bye," I croaked around the knot in my throat before climbing out of the Jeep.

Thanks.

☙❧

DRAKE PICKED ME UP THE NEXT DAY, BUT RATHER THAN TAKING a left out of my community to go to school, he made a right. He never asked. He just assumed I'd be okay with whatever he was doing.

"What's going on? Forget something?" I asked when I realized we were headed toward his house.

"No, just thought we could both use a day off." Okay, so maybe he was right just this one time.

I was excited at the thought of spending an entire day with Drake. No interruptions. No parents sticking their noses in our business.

Drake reached over and took my hand and squeezed it, giving me a goofy smile.

This time, I was prepared for the bumps. I still slid around in my seat, but my death grip on the "oh crap" bar kept me mostly steady. We dodged trees, bouncing over roots, and slid into turns like a motocross racer. Not once did we travel on a road of any kind.

When we came to a stop, I looked at the cabin and couldn't shake the emptiness exuberating from it. It was as if it literally screamed the absence of human life.

"Where's Meliena?"

"At the community college. She likes to take classes every now and then." He gave me the "how did you know she wasn't here" glare. In all honesty, I didn't have a clue. It was just something I sensed.

We both got out of the SUV at the same time, and I followed him around the house. The sky was overcast, but the wind wasn't as fierce as it'd been the past few days. A large barn emerged into view. I couldn't help but quirk my head at the sight of it. What the heck did a Wolf store in a barn? Dinner?

Drake effortlessly opened the massive wooden doors, which I had to admit was kind of hot. I'd expected farm equipment or bales of hay or possibly even animals waiting for their death. I definitely didn't expect to be greeted to a swank car garage. Everything that wasn't a vehicle was encased in chrome. Tools and machines were neatly stored along the walls, and there was a massive black leather couch in the center of the room. For viewing pleasure, maybe? The concrete floor glowed like a recently groomed ice skating rink. The cars on display in the room were shiny, like coins fresh from the mint.

"These are my babies," he said as he crossed his bulging arms with pride.

I had no idea what any of the cars were, but I definitely recognized them as being the best of the best. There were ten vehicles, all in pristine condition. One car looked like it had to be one of the very first cars ever made. It had a button leather bench seat and a crank in the front. The only car I personally recognized by make and model was the newest one, a 2012 Lamborghini. It was bright yellow and looked every bit as fast as it was. I gravitated toward it. The car was all kinds of sexy. I barely breathed for fear of messing something up. The place was seriously cool, and seriously unexpected.

"This is my newest addition." Drake said as he moved to stand right behind me. He wrapped his arms around me, pulling me until my back was snuggled up against his front.

"How in the world can you afford it? Aren't they like two hundred and fifty grand or something like that?" I stood a respectful distance from it.

"Yeah, but you save up a lot of money when you've been on the earth as long as I have," he shrugged. The movement felt weird in this close proximity.

Of course. Maybe he made some smart stock investments?

"Want to test her out?"

"We're in the middle of the woods. She might get a scratch."

"Trust me. She'll be fine."

I bit my lip in indecision as I tilted my head back to look up at him. "I don't know, Drake. Your driveway is pretty rough."

"Who says we're taking the driveway?" He smirked, releasing me to push a button on a panel mounted on the metal wall behind him. A loud pop sounded, and then the floor to our right began to drop. I gasped and jumped back, like a total dork. The ground finally came to a stop, making a ramp leading to an underground tunnel.

"Welcome to my kingdom." He tossed me the keys, which naturally deflected off my hand and crashed onto the floor.

"Way to go, slick," Drake chuckled.

"Hey, you know I'm athletically challenged." I mumbled as I bent to retrieve them.

"Let's take her for a spin." Drake gave me a devilish grin that made my knees go weak.

"I can't drive a stick shift," I panicked, knowing all foreign sports cars were manuals.

"I'm a good teacher."

I scuffed my converses on the pavement to make sure I didn't damage the interior with my muddy feet before getting in the car. I stared blankly at the keyless dash until Drake leaned over and the engine purred to life at the press of a button. I hadn't driven since the accident. The vibrations in my hands as I held onto the wheel both terrified and excited me.

"Now, put the car in first and let up on the clutch. Just ease down the ramp. You'll be fine," he instructed.

The gears crunched and the car lurched forward as I slowly maneuvered us down the ramp. Once the ground leveled out, I braked to take in my surroundings.

We appeared to be in some underground cave. Stalactites and stalagmite speared up and down all around us. The air was cool, and the smell of musky earth tickled my nose.

"Drake, where are we?"

"Just follow the tunnel to the right. I'll explain everything once we get there."

I hesitated as I studied the dark tunnel entrance illuminated only by the car's headlights. I was going to get us killed trying to do this. The car wasn't made for mudding in a cave. And I definitely wasn't coordinated enough to operate a stick shift on dry land, let alone on the highway to Middle Earth.

Drake brought my knuckles up to his lips for a brief kiss. "I have faith in you, Star. Just put her in first and go slow."

I looked into his trusting silver eyes for a few more moments.

Then, on a silent prayer, I shifted into first and the car began to roll.

"Great, isn't it?" Drake asked and squeezed my hand. It was only then that I was aware of our fingers locked and resting on the gear shift. I, of course, made no effort to remove it.

"You have no idea," I sighed and felt a tear slide down my cheek. I might have only been going five miles an hour, but I was finally driving again. God, the freedom!

The tunnel was wider than I originally thought. The cave walls sparkled under the beams of the car's headlights. Several times I caught myself drifting too close to the sides because I was mesmerized by the new world around me.

I gasped in awe as the tunnel opened up and we approached a giant waterfall. My parents took me to see Niagara Falls once when I was seven. As awesome as that sight had been, it paled in comparison to the magnificent view in front of me now. Water flowed from the ceiling of the cave, cascading down rock formations before it landed in a jade green pool at the bottom. Everything looked pure, untouched, untamed.

"Beautiful," I spoke reverently. And to think this was just beneath the surface of Drake's backyard. Gah, I'd never leave if this were mine!

"Yeah, it is."

I tore my eyes off the falls to look at him. He hadn't even been looking at the water. His gaze was solely trained on me.

I cleared my throat before refocusing my attention on the path in front of me. I drove us over natural bridges and under plunging cavern walls until suddenly we were approaching the entrance of a giant, open area.

"You can park here," Drake said, breaking the silence. I put the car in park, cut the engine, and looked around. There were five people sitting, talking to each other. Well, two huddled in opposite corners while the other two seemed to be in some sort of heated debate. In the center of it all was Meliena. What the heck?

"Here, you'll need to give this to Bugsey, she'll be your friend for life."

I looked at the jar of peanut butter he was holding out to me and then back up at him. "Seriously?"

Drake chuckled. "Trust me."

"Who's Bugsey?"

Drake pointed the girl huddled in a corner. "That's her. She's a little skittish around people, but she's cool once you get to know her."

"So, are these your friends?" I asked as I surveyed the small crowd, if a small cluster of five people could even be called that.

"Yep. Come on. It's time you met them."

We both climbed out of the car, and I reluctantly handed Drake the keys in exchange for the jar of peanut butter. As soon as our doors shut, all talking ceased and five pairs of eyes were on us.

"Hey, guys. This is Star. Star, this is the gang." Drake made a quick introduction as we approached them.

I wondered if it was too late to make a run for it.

❧ 22 ❧

❦

Drake

I WATCHED EVERYONE STUDY STAR, EACH TRYING TO DECIDE IF she was someone to be trusted. It didn't matter what I said about her. She had to pass the test before they would open up to her. This meeting was important because they needed to accept that Star was my life now. I'd choose her over them if it came down to it, and they needed to know why firsthand.

"Hi, I'm Stella." It didn't surprise me that Stella was the first to step forward. Of course, she made no move to shake Star's hand. Thankfully, Star seemed to pick up on the silent cue and merely flashed Stella a bright smile.

Please let them like me, she silently pleaded and my heart took a dip in my chest. I hoped so, too.

"Nice to meet you, Stella. I love your hair."

Stella shrugged. "It's genetics. No die in the world gets rid of it."

Rake stepped up next. "I'm Rake. The good-looking one in this bunch." Before Star could say anything, Rake picked her up in a giant hug. My body went rigid at the sight of another man touching her. He plopped her back onto her feet and moved to turn away. Star grabbed a hold of his arm, causing my insides to burst into flames.

"You seem like a nice guy, Rake." Star smiled innocently at him. Rake winked and made a move to disengage himself from her grasp. She *tisked*. "Now, if you'd be so kind as to hand me back my wallet, we can continue as friends and nobody gets hurt."

Sly chortled while Stella rolled her eyes. "Really, Rake? You tried to lift her wallet?"

It happened so fast. I wasn't aware I was moving until I had Rake pressed up against the cave wall, his feet dangling off the ground. My hand squeezed on his windpipe as I growled at him.

"You touch her like that again and I'll have your dead carcass mounted on my wall. Got that?" I tightened my hold until his face turned purple.

"Yeah," Rake wheezed before I tossed him into a heap on the ground. As he huddled down on all fours gasping for air, he retrieved Star's wallet from his back pocket. Star gave him a pat on the back as she took it and stuffed it into her jeans.

"I-I'm S-S-S-Sly." The skunk shifter's face was ten shades of red as he kept his head bowed and hand extended. I silently prayed he'd stay calm.

"It's nice to meet you, Sly. I like your shirt. *The Who* is one of my favorite bands." She shook his hand as she spoke softly.

Sly smiled brightly, briefly making eye contact with her before he released her hand and shuffled back to his corner. "M-mine too."

Odd, seeing him touch her hadn't had the same affect on me. Maybe it had something to do with the fact she initiated it.

Star turned to Bugsey who remained huddled in her corner, frowning at us. I knew Bugsey wasn't a skeptic of Star because of our talk the other day. Unfortunately, her emotions tended to be erratic, so it was possible she could go off on Star for no reason.

"You must be Bugsey. Someone told me this was your favorite." My girl held out the jar of peanut butter.

The squirrel shifter's eyes lit up and she darted forward, grabbing her gift and clutching it to her chest. "Thank you." She hurried back to her corner and proceeded to eat her treat.

I turned to Meliena who was stretched out on an old van seat, her dark brown eyes glowering at me.

Really, Drake? You brought her here? I thought Destiny made it clear where things stood for you.

Instead of replying, I ignored her and focused my attention on Star. "These are some of your nightly protectors."

Star turned to the group and gave them her biggest smile yet. It was a side of her I'd never seen. I was used to snarky Star or melancholic Star or pissed off Star or relaxed Star. I had never seen this care giving side of her. It completely changed her persona, softening her edges, making her trustworthy.

"I'm sorry if I'm messing up your lives. If there was any way to change this mess, I would."

Here's a thought, leave the area and never come back.

I sent a warning in Meliena's direction. *Not. A. Word. Liena.*

She huffed and tossed her braid over her shoulder before standing. "I have class. It was good to see you again, Star."

Before Star had the chance to say anything, Meliena disappeared down one of the dark tunnels. Star slid up beside me and wrapped her arm around my waist. I hugged her against my side as I turned to face the rest of the group.

"It's okay, Star. We know you didn't ask for this." When Stella smiled, her eyes lit up, and she looked so much like her raccoon self that I couldn't hold back my own smile.

"Still," Star frowned, casting her eyes downward.

I gave her shoulders a squeeze, making her train those emerald eyes on me. God, I needed to kiss her. It took a few minutes for me to remember we were still standing in front of my friends. Actually, it took Rake coughing like he had smoker's lung to get my attention.

"The Falcons seem to be keeping their distance. I think we're in the clear for now," Bugsey surprised us all by saying.

Normally, she couldn't be bothered until she finished her peanut butter.

"It's just a rouse. The Falcons aren't the type to sit back," Stella muttered as she pulled out her hand sanitizer and began to furiously clean her hands.

"M-maybe n-no one felt a connection for S-Star and they all l-left." Sly shrugged hopefully.

If only.

I noticed Rake was exceptionally quiet. As the others continued to talk about the Falcons, I tuned into his thoughts, trying to figure out what was up with him today.

He'll flip if I tell him. I'm so screwed.

Unfortunately, he focused his attention on the conversation between Stella and Sly, and I didn't get anything else out of him. What did he have to say that I would be upset about?

"Rake? What do you think?" I asked, hoping he would see this as his opportunity to tell me what was going on.

His eyes shifted around the room at the others before he looked at me. There was a split second where he debated on whether to tell a lie or the truth. I didn't give him the chance to decide. Instead, I grabbed him by the arm and dragged him away from the others.

"Please don't kill me," Rake whispered.

Shit, what had he done?

"Spill it, Rake." I growled as I fisted my hands onto his jacket lapels and pressed him high up against the wall.

He choked and sputtered for a few seconds as his face turned red. His flailing feet connected with my shins but not hard enough to cause any pain.

"I had a little too much to drink at Mike's Bar last night, and um, you know how I get when I'm drunk. I can't shut my mouth and all the truth I normally can't tell starts spilling out. And, well, I might've told Hayden Sterling where Star lived."

"You did what?" I roared as I slammed him into the wall.

"I'm sorry, Drake. I didn't mean to. She was just so hot and came on so strong. I was hopeless, man."

"So you let her lead you around by the dick? You sorry piece of shit!" I threw him down onto the ground. "Doesn't family mean anything to you? You just put us all in jeopardy!"

Rake didn't even try to move. He pulled himself into a fetal position and covered his head, waiting for my next blow. Well, it wasn't going to come. He wasn't worth the mess I'd have on my hands.

"Get out of here. If I catch you in this cave, on my property, or anywhere near Star, I'll kill you."

I didn't wait for him to pick himself up and leave. Instead, I turned and stalked back toward the others. Rake was family. But, Star came first now, and I had to eliminate anyone who would be a threat to her.

When I entered the main room, I found Star sitting in Bugsey's corner with all the others circled around her. Sly and Bugsey weren't their usual jittery messes. Instead, both sat calmly, smiling at whatever Star was saying. Even Stella seemed more stabilized than usual. Not once did she reach for her hand sanitizer or freak over the dirt floor. Star finished speaking and they all erupted with laughter. Our eyes met as she glanced over in my direction, and her smile grew even wider.

You have amazing friends, Drake.

That was true, but she was the most amazing person the Creator ever made. And God help me, I was in love with her.

23

Star

"We like to call this our Island of Misfits." An endearing smile spread across Stella's face.

"What do you mean?" Yeah, there were some things about them that stood out in normal society, but nothing screamed supernatural beings.

"We can't function like normal people. Drake took us in and gave us a safe place to be ourselves."

"You all live in this cave?" My jaw dropped as I looked around at the cold, damp cavern. As much as I said I'd never want to leave this place, no amount of money in the world would get me to *live* down here.

Sly chuckled. "N-no, we each have a c-cabin on the property." He ran his fingers through this short black and white hair. The chunks of white were about two inches wide and ran from his temples to the nape of his neck.

"Oh." That made much more sense.

"Yeah, Drake let us build whatever we wanted, and promised we could stay here as long as we needed." Bugsey smacked her lips after finishing off a glob of peanut butter. If I had to guess, I'd say she was the squirrel shifter. The girl loved her nuts.

"So, what do you do during the day?" I asked, trying to stay focused. These were Drake's friends. I wanted to get to know them and let them know they could trust me. For some reason, that was critically important.

"Sly, Rake, and I are nocturnal, so we mostly sleep during the day," Stella answered.

"And I work out of my house as a copy editor." Bugsey said before she cleaned the last of the jar.

"I work the third shift at a recycling center. We do stuff like turn plastic bottles into yarn and pulping old pencils into paper." Sly added.

"I work nights as a chemical engineer for Y-12." Stella shrugged like it wasn't a big deal. If she had that type of job, the girl had to be a freakin' genius.

They seemed so normal. I had a hard time imagining them as lethal shifters. I'd already figured out Sly was the skunk shifter. The poor guy smelled funky. I wondered if bathing in tomato juice would work for him. I'd have to remember to talk to Drake about that.

Stella was obviously the raccoon based on her silver and black hair and the way she was constantly washing her hands with hand sanitizer. That left Rake as the coyote, but he was MIA at the moment.

I noticed Drake kept himself removed from the group. He sat on an old bench seat watching us. I wanted him to come over and join me but didn't have the guts to send him a blatant invitation. The longer I was around him, the more I craved his touch.

He abruptly stood and stalked away into one of the tunnels. Something was wrong. His body language was screaming at me to comfort him.

"Sorry, I'll be right back," I smiled at everyone before I hopped off my crate and hurried toward where Drake had disappeared.

The light from the main room faded behind me as I struggled to find him.

"Drake?" I called out.

The silence was starting to freak me out and the darker the cave grew, the more claustrophobic I became. I was about to turn back and rejoin the others when a strong hand grabbed a hold of me and pulled me against a warm, solid chest smelling of pine and citrus. A hot mouth pressed against mine, and my world melted away.

He sucked on my bottom lip, and my knees gave out. I gasped as I clung onto his shirt. Drake turned to press my back against the cave wall. With a deep groan, he clamped his large hands down onto my backside and hoisted me up against him. On instinct, I wrapped my legs around his waist, clutching his shoulders for support. Something snapped inside me as I feverishly kissed him back. He rocked his hips forward, making my stomach quiver involuntarily as my body surged with desperate, agonizing need. The kiss reached deep into my core and set my body on fire. I wanted to sink my teeth into his sinful lips and mark him as mine.

"God help me, I tried to stay away but I can't," he gasped as he tore away from my lips and began nibbling down the side of my neck, back to the sensitive spot behind my ear.

I cried out, rocking against him. Nothing. Nothing had ever felt so good. The fabric of his shirt bunched under my fingers.

He kissed me with a drive that both terrified and thrilled me. My chest pressed hard against his, causing amazing friction where I needed it most. He traced the shell of my ear with his tongue before blowing on the moisture. I shivered violently under the pleasure. Everything in me danced to life, and I felt wholly and completely connected with him.

But it wasn't enough.

I needed more. So much more.

"No matter what happens, Star, know that I love you so damn

much," he groaned as he pressed against me before he seized my mouth again. "God, I need you."

I needed him too. If I hadn't lost my ability to speak, I would've told him that. I couldn't say I loved him yet, because I'd learned the hard way that using the L word before you're ready had dire consequences. But, I was definitely in "like" with Drake and could easily see myself one day being wholly, and completely in love with him.

If we were given the chance.

I moved to pull his shirt up, desperately needing to touch his bare skin. He let out a low moan before he pushed me away, setting me back down on my feet.

"Not here," he mumbled before planting a soft kiss on my swollen lips. "Let's go back to the house."

He linked our hands and tugged me forward. As I followed him through the tunnel to where we'd left the car with the others, I couldn't help but think of something that went against every feminist bone in my body: I'd go anywhere as long as he was there to lead me. Could've just been the hormones talking, but I doubted it.

⚜

RON POPE'S "A DROP IN THE OCEAN" FILLED THE SILENCE ON the ride back to Drake's barn. I tried so hard to feel guilty about my growing attraction to him. I really did. But, the result was the exact opposite. In fact, I wanted to climb over the console and maul him as soon as he cut the engine.

But I didn't because I knew the second our lips touched I wouldn't be able to control myself.

"Thank you for letting me into your world," I whispered, not really trusting my voice at the moment.

He gave me a sad smile before unfolding his large frame from the sports car and sauntering over to my side to help me out.

Instead of going straight back to the cabin, we went for a walk in the surrounding woods. He wrapped his arm around my shoulders, and I nestled against him for his warmth. But as sweet as the moment was, I wanted to get back to what we'd been doing in the cave.

"I wish things were different," he sighed.

"What do you mean?"

"I wish I was a normal guy so I could make you mine without worrying about all the damn politics of my world."

"Normal is so overrated."

"You say that now, but wait until the others come into the picture. It's all happening just like it did before. You're going to meet them and your heart will be torn. What will you say when you have three abnormal men fighting for your attention?"

I didn't answer because I couldn't vouch for something that hadn't happened. History might not repeat itself. I could meet the Bear and the Falcon and feel nothing. Then again, I could find something in one of them I needed. Something Drake couldn't provide. I highly doubted that would happen, but I knew it was what he feared...that he wouldn't be enough for me.

He stopped abruptly and turned me so that I was in front of him, staring into his hard eyes.

"I know you can't make a promise for the future, but I can. No matter what happens, I will not live without you in my life, Star. I'll be faithful to you, always. When you die, I die. It's that simple."

My heart ached out of its dormancy, and I felt warmth where I'd been cold for way too long. He lowered his head to mine, and I knew I wanted his kiss more than I wanted my next breath. I closed my eyes, waiting for the connection. His large hand cupped my cheek as his nose caressed mine. He placed small, fluttering kisses on each eyelid, on my cheekbones, along my jaw line. Then, he drew closer, kissing the edges of my mouth but not kissing me where I wanted him most. Just when I was at my breaking point, clutching onto his shirt to keep my knees from buckling, he pulled me against him and took my top lip between his.

I hummed as he slowly proceeded to explore my mouth, leaving nothing untouched. But, as soon as I tried to kick it up a notch, but he pulled back. He pressed his forehead against mine as our mutual panting mingled together.

"God, you're intoxicating." He chuckled as he gulped for air.

"Back at you, wolf boy."

"I need to get you inside before I do something we'll both regret." He linked our hands and led us back to the house.

Once we were inside, he took me to the one place I'd never been: his room. I'd never really pictured Drake sleeping for some reason, but the large king-sized bed with the rumpled sheets told the truth. Everything else was clean and tidy. In fact, the room was sparse. Just a bed, a flat-screen mounted on the wall, a nightstand with a worn copy of *Hard Times* by Charles Dickens and a remote sitting on it, and a black dresser. Nothing else.

Hmm, love the décor. Note to self, give him tons of pictures of us for every special occasion.

Drake smirked but made no apologies or defenses. Instead, he moved quickly to make the bed while I walked over to the large picture window overlooking the property.

"How many acres do you have here?" I asked.

"Two hundred and eleven."

"Huh," I muttered.

"What? Did you think there was more?" He asked as he joined me.

"No. It's just, that's a prime number. I hate prime numbers."

His eyebrows quirked as he gave me a queer look. "Seriously?"

"Yeah. I'd have to sell or buy one acre to make it composite. Probably buy since I like the balance of two-one-two."

He chuckled as he wrapped his arm around me. "You're weird."

I elbowed him in the ribs as I pushed away from him. "Look who's talking, wolf boy."

Drake held his hands up in defeat. "Touché. Are you hungry? I'm sure Meliena left you something edible."

"Sure."

"Okay. You stay here. I'll go see what I can find. Make yourself comfortable." Before I could protest, he was gone.

Since there was nothing other than the TV and the book to occupy my time, I wandered into the bathroom to see what I'd find in there. The sink was clean, unlike mine, and void of any stray hairs or toothpaste scum. The shower was small, taking up only a corner of the room opposite the toilet. I opened the glass door, grabbing the bottle of body soap sitting on the lone ledge. The second I popped the top open, citrus and pine assailed my senses. I was tempted to take it so I'd always have a part of Drake with me, but decided against it. Didn't want him to think I was some creepy stalker more than he already did.

Even though the tile in the shower was still wet, it was clean. Again, no hair clippings or soap residue. I was even more impressed to see the toilet sparkling white inside and out, AND the toilet seat was down. Small miracles.

My favorite part of the bathroom was the Jacuzzi tub. It was big enough to fit two people comfortably and begged me to use it. I resisted...barely, making my way out into the bedroom just as Drake walked in with a tray of sandwiches.

"It's not much, but the bread and cheese are homemade," Drake said as he handed me a plate and a cup of grape juice.

"Trust me, I'm easy to please."

For someone who didn't eat normal-people food, he made one mean sandwich. I ate every last bit of it before taking my first sip of juice. I plopped back onto a pillow on the bed and sighed.

"Did you like it?" He asked as he stretched out beside me. How we both ended up there was anybody's guess, but I wasn't about to move.

"Yes, very much. Thank you." I got brave and gave him a quick peck on the lips. As I began my retreat, however, he anchored me to him with one arm and went in for a longer, deeper kiss. In one swift move, I was on my back as he straddled my thighs. Little grunts rumbled from his chest as I traced my fingers along the waistline of his jeans.

He broke the kiss, burying his face in my neck. His teeth sank into the side of my throat, causing me to cry out as my eyes flew open. God, that was hot! Quickly, his tongue darted out, soothing away the sting, and I begged for him to do it again. And he did. Over and over again.

My hands clawed at his shirt until he got the hint and shed it quickly. For a moment, he paused above me, his eyes wild and dark with desire.

"God, you're so beautiful," he groaned.

He lowered his head, trailing soft kisses from my sternum all the way to the waist of my pants. My back arched. His large hands clamped down onto my hips, holding me in place.

"Drake, please!" I whimpered.

I didn't know what I was asking for. All I knew was I needed him to do something to alleviate the raging fire in my core.

He moved back up my body, reuniting our lips. As our tongues mated, a vision of two toddler girls, one with blonde hair and Drake's silver eyes and the other with red hair and my green eyes, flashed into my mind. *They ran with their chubby arms extended out to me, bright smiles on their little angelic faces. I laughed as I engulfed them in a giant group hug. When I looked up, I found Drake leaning against the doorframe, a big smile consuming his entire face.*

My girls. *I heard him say even though his lips never moved. I could see us through his eyes, mother and her daughters sharing a special moment. My heart swelled as he moved to join us, wrapping us all up in his protective embrace.*

I gasped as I was brought back to reality when Drake bit down on my bottom lip. Did I have a vision or was that my overactive imagination playing tricks on me? Either way, I didn't have time to process it because Drake's wayward hands began to drift south across my stomach, oblivious to whatever happened in my head.

I felt his hardness against my leg, but I wasn't ready for *that*. As wonderful as his mouth was on me, as much as I wanted to sink my teeth into him, I wasn't ready to cross that line yet.

Just before I called a halt to the hot make-out session, Drake stopped, resting his cheek on my stomach.

"You make me lose my mind, Star," he rasped as he ran his hand up to my rib cage and back down to the waistline of my pants.

I weaved my fingers through his hair, enjoying its silkiness, willing my body to cool down.

"Back at you," I grinned up at the ceiling.

"I want to go further. Damn, do I want to go further. But I can't. Once I have a taste of you, I won't be able to stop myself," he groaned as he rolled off me, pulling me onto my side so he could spoon against my back.

"I know. Neither would I," I sighed as I brought his hand to my lips.

He righted me as best as possible before he stood.

"Let's go down to the library. Maybe there I'll be able to control myself."

I took the hand he extended, letting him tug me up onto my feet and out the door. We curled up on the couch, my head resting in his lap as he read Samuel Beckett's *Happy Days* to me.

I was his. Something deep down told me it didn't matter what happened with the others. He was who my heart had chosen.

I spotted his wallet on the coffee table and got a little nosey. Billfolds and wallets were like little windows into a person's soul. Without hesitating, I picked it up and opened it to look at his driver's license.

"Drake Knight, six foot three, blue eyes...twenty-one. Really, Drake? Twenty-one?" I rolled onto my back and raised an eyebrow up at him.

"Hey, just because I have to impersonate a high schooler, doesn't mean I have to avoid the alcohol like one," he chuckled and yanked the wallet away from me before I could look at anything else. But, not before I caught sight of a little black foil package sticking out where he kept his money. The mental image of him putting that bit of latex protection to good use with me knocked the air out of my lungs.

"Makes sense," I cleared my throat, deciding we needed a distraction before I threw myself at him. His scent was fogging my brain, and all I wanted to do was lick every mound and crevice on his body.

It suddenly felt like I was lying on a big stick. I frowned before my eyes grew huge with awareness. My cheeks flushed hot as I glanced up at him only to see his sheepish grin.

"You think like that and it's going to cause a reaction." He shrugged.

"Have you ever been, you know, active with anyone else?" I heard myself asking.

He squinted down at me, as if he was trying to choose his words wisely. "Depends on what you consider active."

"Have you had sex?"

"No."

"Seriously?" I raised my eyebrows in surprise. "How is that possible? You've been on this earth forever."

Drake sighed as he rubbed his hands over his face. "This is not a conversation I want to have with you."

"Well, you need to since we almost made it to second base in your bedroom."

He studied me for a second before his shoulders slumped. "Fine. I can't have sex until I'm married. It's a Guardian law."

"Why doesn't that surprise me?" I snorted. The goodie goodie shifters would be the ones to make a law prohibiting sex before marriage.

"It's not because we're *goodie goodies*." He tweaked my nose. "It's a law meant to prevent us from creating armies of shifters for evil."

"I thought you could only turn your mates."

"Having sex is mating, Star." He eyed me like I had a screw loose.

"I mean your spouse, soul mate, whatever."

"We'll change our partners regardless of a marriage license."

"Why would the Creator do that?"

"Because sex isn't supposed to be taken lightly. Whenever someone sleeps with someone, a soul connection is made, even if just for a moment. The connection is usually deeper for shifters because we mate for life."

"But why have a rule, then? If you mate for life, wouldn't you only be attracted to your mate?"

"Because we're also human, and a fine ass is a fine ass." He smirked.

I shoved him, rolling my eyes. "Okay. So, what happens if you break the rules?"

"You're kicked out of *The Guardians*. Most end up joining *Shadowmen* if they haven't already. We've only had one case where someone was sentenced to *Shadowmen* because he created a militant group of shifters."

"An army of female shifters. Interesting," I snorted.

"They weren't all female." He eyed me.

"Gottcha."

"Are we done with this awkward conversation?"

"Why?"

A wicked grin spread on his face right before his fingers ran along my stomach, sending me into a wreathing, squealing, giggling heap.

When my hand grazed his abs by mistake, he grunted, "Hey, none of that."

"You're ticklish, too!" I cried with delight. "Oh, it's on!"

And so the great tickle war began.

Meliena chose to enter the living room the exact moment when I was straddling Drake's hips, my fingers under his shirt as he held my foot hostage. I wasn't sure how we twisted ourselves into that position, but judging by the stern look on Meliena's face, she wasn't amused.

"Hey, I picked up some salad," she said as she walked further into the room.

I tried to roll off Drake but he held me in place.

"Good. How did class go?" He asked, as if I wasn't using him as a chair

"We talked about irrigation," her nose turned up in obvious distaste.

She stood there in silence, and I realized they were communicating with their minds.

"Hey, so not fair," I huffed.

"Meliena was warning me not to get too attached," Drake said, not pulling his gaze from his sister's.

"And Drake was just reminding me things can change. Look, honestly, Star." Meliena broke her stare war with Drake and turned to lay the full force of her large brown eyes on me. They were much too big to be normal. "I think you're great, but you won't pick Drake."

"You chose a Wolf," I pointed out.

"I didn't have a choice," she huffed and left the room.

I bit my lip, certain I'd just ruined things between her and me.

"She'll get over it. She hasn't completely let go of John. He was trying to protect me and one of the Falcons got him. There was nothing any of us could do."

"Is that why she stays around you?"

He nodded sadly.

"I think she can't fully accept that he'd fulfilled his purpose on earth. They'd only been married for a year when he died."

"His purpose was to die protecting you."

He winced as he released my foot. The lighthearted mood we'd finally settled into was gone.

"Maybe, but what neither of us can figure out is while she didn't die shortly after. Once one mate dies, the other will follow shortly after. It's the natural progression of things."

"Is it possible to have two mates?"

"It's never been done before."

"Then, I guess God's not finished with her yet."

He smiled at me before leaning up to cup my face, taking my

mouth hostage. I forgot all about what we'd been talking about, focusing everything on him.

All too soon, he put a halt to the heavy kissing.

"I need to call your parents and let them know you're staying for dinner," Drake said as he grabbed his phone and dialed my home number. I didn't even want to know how he got that since I'd never given it to him.

Surprisingly enough, Mom seemed okay with us being at his house.

The gang minus Rake showed up and we ate salad. Well, Stella, Drake, Meliena, Sly, and I ate salads while Bugsey ate a bowl of mixed nuts. Eventually, Meliena warmed up enough to talk about her day.

After dinner, we played a game of Nertz, which was really just the games of solitary and speed on crack. At one point, I was afraid we were all going to die when Stella slipped her three of hearts down onto a two of clubs just as Sly was doing the same, beating him to the punch. His face turned red and his slender frame began to shake violently.

"It's okay, Sly," Drake intervened, patting his friend on the shoulder. I watched the skunk shifter take in a few deep breaths before nodding, his face returning to normal.

Shew, crisis diverted.

I didn't want Drake to drive me home, but it was a school night. Plus, I knew Mom's leniency with Drake would only stretch so far. As much as fun as I'd had with Drake and his family, I couldn't shake the feeling that the happiness I had was nothing but a mirage. Something dark was on the horizon.

"Thanks for going along with today," he said and placed a kiss on my forehead, making me feel cherished. "I hope you get all your answers one day. It would make your thoughts calm down."

He chuckled, but it lacked any merriment. I smiled sadly as I waited for him to get out and come over to help me down from the Jeep. We walked up to my front door and stood there awkwardly for a few minutes.

"I'll probably go to hell for this," he growled and cupped my face in his big hands and pressed my back against the wall. His lips descended over mine and his tongue forced its way into my mouth. Every intense emotion he felt poured into his kiss, and I was powerless to do anything else but respond with equal passion. I rose up on my toes and delved my fingers into his hair, wishing it was still long so I could grab it. He moaned into my mouth as his hands dropped to my waist so he could mesh our lower halves together. Way too many layers were between us, and I wanted them gone.

The porch light flicked on, causing him to jump back and dry-wash his fingers through his hair. "I love you, Star," he whispered before he leapt off the porch and jumped into his Jeep.

I numbly turned and walked inside. Glancing out the window, I caught him sitting behind the wheel with his head resting on his hands. His shoulders heaved before he straightened, stared at my house for what felt like forever, started the engine, and drove off.

I brought my trembling fingers to where I could still feel him on my lips. That kiss had been nothing like any of the others today. I couldn't shake the feeling tonight's kiss on the front porch felt like a goodbye.

❧ 24 ❧

❀

Star

ONYX DECIDED A SLEEPOVER AT HER HOUSE WAS THE PERFECT
way to spend our Friday night. I dreaded it. All they'd do was talk
about boys while doing each other's nails. But, Drake seemed
pleased with the arrangement. Every time I complained to him
about it, he'd just smile, kiss my temple, and tell me I might be
surprised at how much fun I had. As if.

A huge smile spread on his face when he spotted my backpack
stuffed with pajamas, a change of clothes, and the essential
toiletries Friday morning.

"Are you ready to ace your Spanish test?" he asked.

"Nope." I emphasized the "p" sound and saw a little spittle fly
out my mouth. That was classy.

He kissed my hand before driving us to school. The moment I
saw my two jail wardens in the hallway, I contemplated making a
run for it.

"Be good," Drake whispered in my ear as he wrapped his arm around my waist, holding me hostage.

I glowered up at him. All he did was chuckle and kiss my nose before releasing me.

"See you in band." He waved before disappearing into the crowd of people shuffling off to their respective classes.

Onyx and Wayley talked non-stop about their plans for the night. Ideas such as having a photo shoot to rolling someone's house were tossed in the air. I voted "no" for both, but they ignored me. When I gave Wayley the liberty to decide on what to do for the night, it obviously meant abdicating the ability to have any say on the matter.

After school, Drake walked me out to Wayley's little VW Bug.

"You know how to reach me," he spoke lowly as he held me in his arms.

"We could skip all this 'goodbye' mess and do something together tonight," I suggested hopefully.

"We never say, 'goodbye.' Only 'see you later.'" He murmured before his lips pressed lightly against mine. I wanted to latch on and take a deep drink of him, but he released me and spun me around to face the girls.

"Take care of her," he eyed Wayley.

Wayley gave a playful glare. "She'll be fine, Mr. Overprotective. Now shoo, we've got girls' night to get to."

I reluctantly climbed into the car. He stayed where I'd left him. Our eyes locked, and I shuttered at the haunted expression on his face. It was as if he was torn between doing the right thing and what his heart was telling him to do. I gave him a small smile as Wayley drove us away from the school. I didn't tear my eyes away from the window until he was out of sight. I couldn't shake the ominous feeling in my veins.

Onyx's parents' house was much larger than Wayley's and mine combined. Located in a subdivision off Seymour's main highway, it displayed all the wealth and class obviously embedded in the community. It was a Spanish-style home with tan stucco, heavy wood trim, and clay curved roof tiles. There were large arches on the windows and the front porch. One of the arched windows contained some sort of stained glass while the others were as large as a feature window in a normal house. The yard was perfectly manicured and dotted with evergreen trees and plants to give it color despite the deadness of winter.

"What do your parents do?" I asked, stunned. Even my parents' house in Atlanta hadn't been this nice, and we'd been well-off back then.

"My dad is a chemical engineer for Y-12 and my mom is working on a special program for NASA. She travels back and forth between here and Florida almost every day." Onyx shrugged as if it was nothing to be the product of two insanely smart parents.

Inside the mansion ran the same Spanish theme. The rooms were spacious with arched walkways and exposed wooden beams. Colorful tile spread out under our feet and occasionally on the walls. Bright paintings and wrought iron works were strategically placed throughout the house. Votive lights and candles twinkled in little corners.

The living room was complete with a massive flat screen TV and stacks of DVDs and Blu-rays displayed on glass shelves.

"Oh, pooh. It looks like we're gonna have to make a run to the store," Onyx said as she walked in from the humongous kitchen. I hadn't even realized she'd left us.

Looking around at her living room, I suddenly felt self-conscious about my little house. What had they thought when they saw all the mix-matched furniture and the lack of any decorative theme?

"That's fine. I need to drop something off at the post office anyway," Wayley shrugged.

We tossed our things in Onyx's room, which was decked in black and red; not pink, thank God. Then we piled into Onyx's little car. At the store, Onyx was a girl on a mission. Her dark brown ponytail bounced with every step she took. Whenever she saw what she needed, she grabbed it, tossed it into the buggy, and then moved on to the next section. Wayley kept pointing to items on the shelves and talking about how she'd either tried it and hated it or tried it and couldn't live without it. I wanted us to get the heck out of there. I hated grocery stores. Something to do with the overwhelming selection to choose from.

"My, don't you look just like your mother!" A woman who'd been looking at the soups declared as she turned to me.

"Huh?" I asked, completely caught off guard. I'd been staring hard at the shrimp flavored Ramen Noodles, trying to figure out who would ever willingly eat dehydrated shellfish.

"You must be Elizabeth, Victoria's daughter."

Since when did Mom have friends? And just who the hell did this woman think she was calling me "Elizabeth?"

I smiled awkwardly and tried to keep on walking, but she obviously wasn't finished talking. "Vicki talks about you all the time. How's that problem going with the boy who died? Getting any better? Honey, trust me when I say I've been there. Poor dear."

I was absolutely mortified. My mother had been talking about my Clint situation to other people! With a huff, I stomped passed the woman, leaving Onyx and Wayley no choice but to scurry behind me like baby ducks following their mother.

"What did she mean?" Onyx asked once we were out of ear-shot.

"I don't know," I lied. As soon as I had a moment to myself, I was calling my mother. I wanted some answers.

"Hey, yer Tommy's girl, ain't ye?" a rather rich-accented guy exclaimed. I turned to see a man dressed in blue coveralls and a black toboggan rolled up like a beanie walking over to us.

Rather than responding, I kept walking muttering, "Stupid people, stupid store, stupid town."

Onyx hurried to get the remaining items on her list, and we made a quick detour to the post office before heading back to her house. Apparently the grocery store was the place to be seen, and my parents were frequent visitors. I made a mental note to never go in that store again.

Once we were safely at Onyx's, the "party" began. I was tortured into letting them paint my nails a crimson red and style my hair into various poor attempts of the latest fashion. I tried to explain how it had a mind of its own, but they were determined to find a better look for me. Apparently, my unruly waves weren't currently in style.

The entire night I kept shouting mental threats to Drake, hoping he was hearing my thoughts and realizing how much torture I was going through for him.

I'm going to paint your nails when I get a hold of you, wolf boy!

Around eight that night, Onyx's dad came home. He smiled at us and said anything in the fridge was ours before going off to his room on the opposite side of the house.

"He's been coming home really tired lately. Some weird things have been happening at the lab," Onyx said as she munched down on a celery stick.

"What kind of things?" I asked, my instincts telling me this was somehow related to Drake's absence. There was a chance it wasn't, but all my nerves said otherwise.

"I'm not really sure, but I overheard him telling Mom they lost three security guards. All of them were mutilated. Nothing appears to have been stolen, but someone obviously wants inside. They're worried someone might be planning to tamper with the reactors."

"Do you think maybe an animal did it?" Wayley asked.

"I don't know. Dad hasn't told me himself what's going on. Apparently, they're trying to keep the media out of it until they figure it out. I'm assuming my ignorance is for my own good."

Do you know what's going on?

I knew I wasn't going to get a response from him. The air was shifting around me, as if something in the universe just fell into place. I know *I* was somehow related to those Y-12 incidences.

"You know my dad is chief of police for Sevier County,

right?" Wayley barely gave us enough time to respond before continuing, "Well, he told my mom there has been a series of animal attacks lately that are like nothing he's ever seen. The victims are really maimed but not a drop of blood is spilt on the ground. Strange, right?" Wayley said through a mouthful of carrot.

Drake, please tell me what's going on! This is really freaking me out!

My phone went off, and I pulled it out of my pocket to see the text message was from him.

TRUST ME.

The only thing the message did was confirm my suspicion that he was involved in all of it.

"Was that from Drake?" Onyx smiled knowingly.

"No," I lied again.

"I think that boy is head over heels for you." She winked at me.

"Let's hope so, if he's going to spend that much time with her and kiss her like that. Mmm, mmm." Wayley sighed. "God, he's so sexy."

"Can't girls have friends who're guys but not boyfriends?" I asked; irritated at the attention he was getting.

"Sure, but he looks at you differently than a friend should," Onyx shrugged.

"And friends don't kiss like that," Wayley added. She was obsessed with that damn kiss!

I wasn't about to give them the low-down.

Thankfully, Onyx changed the subject when I didn't respond, and they moved back to talking about themselves again. Thank God!

I endured the rest of the night, but more than anything, I just wanted to see Drake and talk to him about what was going on. Who or what was attacking these people? And did it have anything to do with me?

Once we finally settled down for the night, I had a hard time falling asleep. My thoughts were all jumbled, and I just wanted

Drake to be there to hold me. God, my muscles ached with need for his touch. It wasn't normal!

An hour after we said our goodnights, I heard Onyx rustling in her sleeping bag. I watched as she slipped out of the room. A few seconds later, the shower started. I guess she couldn't sleep either.

Yawning, I rolled onto my stomach and finally drifted off to sleep dreaming about Drake.

25

Drake

I CROUCHED IN THE BUSHES, WATCHING AS TWO FIGURES IN black ran through the woods. The interrogations had been successful. The kid was a freshman at Walters State and told us anything we wanted to know the second he realized Mack was the sheriff. As it turned out, the *Purists* weren't made by accident. They had help. Shadowmen. Tonight, they were planning another raid on the plant, trying to make it look like we were to blame.

I'd been too late the last few times, but I'd get them now.

Gottcha, I grinned before I took off after them. They were humans on foot, making it easy to stay on their trail without getting too close. Finally, they came to a stop in front of an old abandoned building.

Neither spoke until they got inside, thinking they were safe. Stupid humans.

"Did you learn anything?" An unfamiliar voice asked.

"No, except that she's definitely seeing him." My ears twitched with recognition. I knew the second person. A female. But both their thoughts were empty, so I couldn't delve in to try to get any more clues.

"Do you have a plan?" The first person asked.

"It's already in motion. By tomorrow night, Star will forget all about her precious mutt," the familiar one replied.

I grunted, not liking the feeling in my chest. *I'll kill you before you touch her.*

"Why didn't you call a group meeting, then?"

"Because I'm the leader. I can do whatever I want." *You're dead, bitch.*

The wind picked up, shifting slightly, and I caught the scent of cinnamon and leather.

My muscles tensed, preparing to take off when two sets of talons dug into my back, lifting me off the ground. I howled with pain as I fought to disengage myself from their grasp. As desperate as I was to break away, I couldn't help but be pissed that I hadn't heard them above me in the trees.

Whoever held me captive flew into the side of the building, throwing me against a steel beam. Stars flashed in my eyes as I was dropped onto the ground. All the air escaped my lungs as I slammed hard onto my side.

As I struggled to regain my balance and clear my vision, I saw four bodies hover over me. The two in black were closest while the Falcons stayed back at a distance, probably afraid I'd identify them.

"Well, well, lover boy. How nice of you to join us." I squinted, desperately trying to see who the familiar voice belonged to.

"Stake him to the ground," she commanded.

The Falcons moved toward me, large iron posts captured between their talons. I tried to get up, but my body wasn't cooperating. Several ribs were cracked. But I didn't feel it, because my only focus was on my captors. Their eyes flashed red and one let out a sharp cry before the two rods were thrust into my side, deep into the concrete floor, anchoring me to the ground. Howls and human screams erupted from my chest as my body shimmered between man and Wolf. I could feel all my energy flowing toward the wounds, struggling to heal them, but the presence of the poles made it impossible.

I grunted as I desperately tried to dislodge myself. I didn't care if I lost half my body in the process, I couldn't stay pinned down. Finally, I settled into my human form, shaking violently as I tried to overpower the burning, hot pain consuming me.

My only thought was that I had to save Star. God, I'd rather die than let something happen to her.

"Aw, he's crying."

I turned my head as I clenched my jaw in an effort to show a calm I didn't feel. A phone went off, the light reflecting off the speaker's face. My eyes grew wide with recognition.

"Oh, shit."

"Surprise," she smirked.

✿ 26 ✿

༺❀༻

Star

Saturday wasn't my favorite day. Cold, hard rain fell like sheets of glass onto the ground, and I was forced to stay inside. Mom and Dad went to some meeting before I got home, so I couldn't demand answers from them about the people I met in the store. I'd finished all my homework, none of my books sounded appealing, and most importantly, Drake hadn't called or stopped by.

To keep from going crazy, I decided to go on a cleaning spree. Dusting, vacuuming, organizing, and polishing every square inch of my room.

Once my room was sparkling, I drifted into the living room, curled up on the blue, red, and green plaid sofa and stared at the TV. I could care less about what was on TV, so I kept it off, choosing instead to mentally try to work through the puzzle that had become my life. At the moment, the only piece I could see was

Drake's, and it was fuzzy, like I was holding it an inch away from my face.

There was a rap on the living room window. Excitement surged through me as I jumped out of the sofa and ran to it. The second my eyes landed on a drenched Meliena shivering on the other side of the glass, my heart stopped. I motioned her to the backdoor and charged through the house to open it. She fumbled in, shaking. Her lips were blue and her black hair hung in thick clumps, sticking to her high cheekbones. She looked like a drowned puppy.

"What is it?" I asked, dreading the answer.

"W-water," she rasped.

I ran into the kitchen and filled a glass of water up to the rim. Half of it sloshed onto the floor as I dashed back to her, but I didn't really care. After she downed the glass, she slumped down onto a dining room chair and stared at the floor.

"Meliena, what's going on? You have to tell me." I was kneeling in front of her, clasping on to her trembling legs.

"H-he said he wouldn't get caught," she whispered so softly I almost missed the words.

"Drake? Where is he? Is he okay?" Panic crept into my voice, and I feared I was going to be imitating her in a few short moments.

"He said if he wasn't back by morning to come over here. I had to look for him first." She was still rambling. I resisted the urge to slap her to get her to focus.

"Meliena, you have to tell me what's going on."

"He's gone. I can't believe he's gone."

"What? What do you mean *gone?*"

"It's the only explanation. They got him."

"They? They who. Snap out of it! I need you to focus!"

"He said he wouldn't get caught," she repeated herself. Damn it, she was in shock!

"Snap out of it, Meliena. Where is Drake?"

Meliena began to tremble as the words fumbled from her lips, "He's gone, Star. Drake's gone."

Pain like I'd never experienced sliced into my heart, exploding out at my sides. I doubled over, struggling hard to keep myself together. A tidal wave of emotion was building, and God, I didn't think I was going to survive it.

ABOUT THE AUTHOR

As a child, K.R. Grace had an overactive imagination. When it was obvious she wasn't going to change anytime soon, her mom shoved a pen and paper in her hand and said, "Write it down." So, at the age of eight, her first story was born, and the writing hasn't stopped since. When she's not running with wolves, sleeping with bears, or flying with falcons, she can be found checking out local bands or watching movies about things that go "boo" in the night. She has a dog that is afraid of his own shadow and a cat that was a mob leader in a former life.

K.R. wants to hear from you, the reader. You can find her at the following:
    www.facebook.com/KRGraceAuthor
    www.twitter.com/KRGrace10
    www.pinterest.com/KRGrace10
    k.r_grace_author@yahoo.com

ALSO BY K.R. GRACE

www.ingramcontent.com/pod-product-compliance
Lightning Source LLC
Chambersburg PA
CBHW070109260626
47160CB00004B/1394